Laughing and sputtering water, she crashed against his chest while his back hit the sandy bottom

"You're horrible!" Stephanie said, still laughing and clinging to Brady for balance. She felt amazing against him. Curvy. Wet. Hot.

On autopilot, he did what any sane guy would, and kissed her. Hands loose on her hips, warm water swirling at his feet, he tilted his head to get better access, which she granted. She tasted sweet—forbidden. Her breathy moans only made him want her more.

Suddenly, she drew back, her expression dazed, and she put her hands to her lips. "Oh, no..." Awareness of what they'd just done brightened her eyes and she looked almost as panicked as she had on the plane.

Brady struggled to remain calm. "Sorry. I don't know what came over me. It won't happen again."

Dear Reader,

Not gonna lie—this book was tough! The research was a little trickier than normal, the level of household teen drama going on while writing was through the roof and not just one or two characters had tough issues to work through, but *everyone* in the story! With all of those problems, there were times I wanted to take the manuscript and fling it from the deck!! But then I thought about how much cleaning that would entail when the yard committee noticed over two hundred pieces of paper littering our yard!

All kidding aside, fresh from reading the latest draft, I got a little teary. Far from despising, loathing and hating these people, I now loved them—emotional baggage and all.

Which leads me to my point... This book took me out of my comfort zone. As I get older, it's not a place I like to be, yet when I manage to stumble in, I always come out stronger for having made the trip. In real life, I'm not a risk taker. I don't bungee jump or even change brands of toilet paper. But with this story, the long-forgotten daredevil in me wanted to come out to play. Nobody in this book literally skydives, but I think that sometimes really brave emotional decisions are even harder than physical challenges. I know Brady and Stephanie would agree!

Happy reading!

Laura Marie

The Baby Twins
LAURA MARIE ALTOM

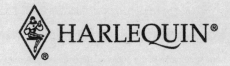

HARLEQUIN®

TORONTO • NEW YORK • LONDON
AMSTERDAM • PARIS • SYDNEY • HAMBURG
STOCKHOLM • ATHENS • TOKYO • MILAN • MADRID
PRAGUE • WARSAW • BUDAPEST • AUCKLAND

Recycling programs
for this product may
not exist in your area.

ISBN-13: 978-0-373-75309-3

THE BABY TWINS

ABOUT THE AUTHOR

After college (Go, Hogs!), bestselling, award-winning author Laura Marie Altom did a brief stint as an interior designer before becoming a stay-at-home mom to boy/girl twins and a bonus son. Always an avid romance reader, she knew it was time to try her hand at writing when she found herself replotting the afternoon soaps.

When not immersed in her next story, Laura teaches art at a local middle school. In her free time, she beats her kids at video games, tackles Mount Laundry and of course reads romance!

Laura loves hearing from readers at either P.O. Box 2074, Tulsa, OK 74101, or e-mail BaliPalm@aol.com.

Love winning fun stuff? Check out www.lauramariealtom.com!

Books by Laura Marie Altom

HARLEQUIN AMERICAN ROMANCE

*U.S. Marshals
**Baby Boom

For Nancy Blattner—flight attendant extraordinaire!
Thanks for so frankly—and quickly—answering the
questions no one else would touch. You're a doll!

And for pilot James K. Durden, my old Springdale
High School friend and new Facebook friend—
I can't thank you enough for patiently leading me
through years of flight school in under an hour.

Please know that any and all errors
in this story are all mine.
The good stuff should be credited to Nancy and James.

Chapter One

"…In preparation for takeoff, the captain has requested that all seat backs and trays be returned to…"

Clutching the armrests of seat 24C, Stephanie Olmstead forced a deep breath. Heart racing, mouth dry, she told herself she was being ridiculous for worrying about the flight. She'd flown dozens of times. Had friends who were pilots. Her husband had been a navy pilot. After leaving the military, he'd worked for TransGlobal Airlines. He'd joined the Air National Guard. Went to Iraq. Never came home. Michael had told her that statistically, she was much safer on a plane than in her minivan. But if that were true, why was he dead?

"First time flyer?" the middle-aged man seated beside her asked while frenetically tapping away on his BlackBerry. He wore a rumpled gray suit that matched his equally rumpled hair. His musky cologne churned the blueberry bagel and OJ she'd hastily downed for breakfast.

"No," she managed. Though the September temperature in Little Rock had been in the uncharacteristic blustery fifties, the plane's interior had grown stiflingly warm as they'd sat waiting in Memphis to begin the second leg of their journey. Thank goodness she'd left her twins in the capable hands of friends, Olivia and Tag O'Malley. Her girls were prone to heat rash.

"We'll be fine," he assured her, ignoring a flight attendant's request to turn off cellular devices. "I'm a bag dragger. Do this all the time. Where you headed?"

"Miami." Why wouldn't he leave her alone? At least the row's middle seat was empty. If she'd had to be crushed up against the guy, she'd probably be even more uneasy. Her twin sister wanted to be with her, but she hadn't been able to leave work when Michael's friend Austin had made his request, leaving Stephanie to go on a solo mission.

"Duh," the guy said with a snort. "Every danged one of us is gonna end up in Miami. I mean, after that. Convention? Vacation? Work?"

"Tying loose ends," she said, hoping her curt tone conveyed that she wasn't in the mood for chitchat. "Concerning my dead husband."

"Oh." After finally turning off his phone, he said, "I was just at a cousin's wake. Damnedest thing you ever did see. He was a huge Dallas Cowboys fan, and right there on his casket was—"

"If you don't mind," Stephanie said over the MD-90's engine's roar, "I—I'd like to try getting some rest."

"Good luck." From the seat pocket in front of him, he withdrew a detective novel and a yellow bag of Peanut M&M's. "I never can sleep a wink on these tin cans. I like the big boys. Used to be when a man flew—"

"Please," Stephanie implored, the force of takeoff pressing her back in her seat, "if you could just be quiet, I'd appreciate it."

The man shot her a put-out glare before launching a conversation with the grandmotherly sort sitting across the aisle.

Blessedly alone in her private hell, Stephanie tried working through the steps her doctor had suggested for fending off a full-blown panic attack. Ever since Michael's unexpected death, she'd been plagued by the "buggers" as longtime friend and physician, Naomi, had dubbed the frightening incidents.

No one has ever died from a panic attack, Stephanie chanted three times in her head. The coping statement was supposed to make the stressful time easier, but in this case, the higher the plane climbed, the worse she felt.

Tugging at the collar of the white T-shirt she wore beneath a black velour jogging suit, she told herself the cabin wasn't abnormally hot. Even so, she wrangled free of her long-sleeved jacket.

Her throat felt closed off, and it was growing increasingly hard to breathe.

Naomi had prescribed medication for just this sort of thing, but being a single mom of nine-month-old twin girls, the last thing Stephanie wanted to do was not be alert when her babies needed her.

Twenty minutes into their journey, a flight attendant stopped the drink cart at the end of the row. "Would either of you care for a complimentary beverage or—"

"Gimme a gin and tonic and one of those cans of chips." Stephanie's seatmate handed the blonde a ten. "Keep the change, cutie."

The woman thanked him for the offer, but returned his change. "Ma'am?" she asked Stephanie. "May I get anything for you?"

A new body?

Stephanie shook her head.

Eyes stinging, she followed Naomi's advice to breathe slowly through her nose. When that didn't help, she tried more coping statements. *I can be anxious and still deal with this situation. All I have to do is close my eyes and wait for this to pass.*

Yeah, right.

Now clawing at her T-shirt, Stephanie knew she was on the edge of a dangerous place. *Hot, so hot.* If she could just get fresh air—away from the musky cologne—then maybe she could breathe.

She tried standing, but her seat belt blocked the way.

"Helps if you unbuckle it first," her neighbor said with a gin-laced chuckle.

"I have to get out of here," she said, yanking at her seat-belt buckle, and finally freeing herself only to encounter her seatmate's tray table. In her haste, she crashed into it, sending his drink flying all over his lap and the floor. "I have to get out of here."

"What the hell?" he complained, stowing his tray table before getting up to brush himself off.

She was going to be sick, and not caring if she caused the man further inconvenience, she ran to the back of the plane, aiming for the lavatory. The flight attendant's cart blocked her way. "I—I have to get off this plane," she said in a rush. "Michael died in the air and his body was never found and I know he burned in the explosion and I can't stand the thought of him that way and—" She was crying so hard, so hysterically, that her words stopped coming out.

She closed her eyes, willing herself back to her safe home, away from the horrific images that'd haunted her ever since her husband's death.

"Let's get this stowed," an attendant said, already moving backward.

"I have to get off this plane!" Stephanie screamed.

Running down the aisle, toward the front exit door, Stephanie tripped, but then was back on her feet. She wouldn't—*couldn't*—die this way. She'd been entrusted with raising Michael's daughters and she refused to let him down.

A man lunged for her, but Stephanie dodged him.

"I don't want to die! I don't want to burn." Present merged with the past—Michael's past. Her lungs felt raw from a lack of air. If she could only get outside—into the sun.

She'd just reached the front exit, and had her hand on the latch, when the cockpit door opened and out came a uniformed pilot.

"Michael?" she asked, having difficulty seeing through tears. "Please, you have to help get this open!"

"Zip tie her hands!" someone shouted. "She'll kill us all."

Everywhere people stared and pointed and talked all at once. Why wouldn't they stop? Or at least help her get away?

"Michael, please," she cried, "if you'd just help me go outside, then I could be with the girls and everything would be—"

"Steph?" After shaking off a bewildered expression, he slipped into professional mode. "I'm sorry," Michael said in a warm, yet firm tone, taking her hands, leading her away from the exit. "Hercules himself couldn't open this door midflight, but for your safety, as well as that of everyone else on board, I can't have you running wild."

"Are you taking me to another door?" she asked, her tear-filled eyes seeing him silhouetted in a golden glow. "I love you, Michael. Thank you for saving me. If I could just get a breath, I'll be okay."

"I know," he said, wrapping a cold plastic tie around her wrists and pulling it tight. "It won't be much longer and you'll have all the outside air you need. But up here, I'm afraid you're out of luck."

"You don't understand," she implored, crying all the harder now that he was leading her away from the light. "I can't die up here. I have to get home to my babies."

"No one's dying today," he said, urging her into a plush leather first-class seat.

"Oh, that's great," a disgruntled voice said. "All you have to do for an upgrade is threaten to kill everyone on board?"

"She did no such thing," said another voice. "She's clearly in a lot of pain, and—"

"Hush it with the touchy-feely garbage," said a more familiar tone, "she owes me a new drink. I knew she was a fruitcake from the second she sat down."

"If the pilot's out here," yet another voice asked, "who's flying?"

"These people hate me," Stephanie said. "See? They want me to get off the plane."

"Tie her legs!" a shrill woman shouted.

The pilot barked to a flight attendant, "Get them in their seats. I want no one within three rows."

"Yes, Captain."

An angry male said, "I paid for a first-class seat, and by God, no one's telling me, I—"

"Move," the pilot commanded, "or the second we land, I'll have you arrested." He sat in the seat beside Stephanie and fastened her safety belt. In a gentler tone, he asked, "Don't you know who I am?"

"You… You're Michael." As if in a dream, Stephanie

tried cupping his dear cheek, but with her hands restrained, she couldn't quite reach. "I've missed you so much."

"I'm sorry," he said, "but, honey, I'm Brady. Remember? Brady McGuire. Clarissa's husband. When you and Michael lived in Dallas, we used to all hang out together?"

With a sniffle, she nodded. Dawning had been slow to come, but once it had, she wished for a rock to crawl under.

"Remember those crappy apartments by Burger Palace?" Chuckling, he shook his head. "While you and Clarissa gossiped, Michael and I shot hoops on that weed-choked court."

She still found it hard to breathe, but she nodded in hopes of making her old friend go away. "He hated losing."

"Me, too." Sobering, he added, "Michael was a good guy. He had a lot of friends at TransGlobal. You need to know that…"

Gaze darting, she saw the carpeted orange, blue and brown design on the bulkhead. The leather seats. Earth 33,000 feet below. Her pulse had slowed, but her stomach still churned.

"Stephanie? Do you know where you are?"

"Of course." Toying with the dangling end of the plastic around her wrists, she asked in a quiet tone, "Could you please cut these off? They hurt."

"Sorry." His smile was sincere. "You caused quite a stir, and even though we go back a long way, I'm afraid you're under house arrest."

Her mind's eye flashed to herself trying to open the cabin door. Humiliation didn't begin to cover the emotions coursing through her. Though physically painful, she brought her hands to her face, crying again, but for different reasons now. She was no longer frightened, but exhausted to a degree she'd never dreamed possible.

"Hey…" Brady awkwardly patted her shoulder. "Relax. Crisis averted. Stay put until we get to Miami, answer a few questions for the nice TSA gentleman, and you'll be on your way."

"A-am I going to jail?"

"I don't think so," he said, "but the air-travel climate these days is tricky."

"I'm a mess," she said.

"Understandable. I'll do everything I can to diffuse the situation."

"Th-thank you." As much as her husband had despised losing to the man in basketball, Michael had thought highly of Brady. He'd always said he was a great pilot and even better friend. Luck was shining down on her for him to be on board.

After a sharp exhale, he said, "Well, I should get back to the controls. You going to be all right if I leave you with Amanda? She's the flight attendant assigned to your seat."

"I'm good," Stephanie lied.

"GLAD TO SEE YOU IN ONE PIECE." Craig, Brady's copilot, made a notation on the flight log.

"Me, too. We don't get paid enough for this kind of stuff."

"Panic attack?"

"A doozy." Since 9/11, they'd been more common. "And you won't believe who it was."

"Lay it on me."

"Michael Olmstead's widow."

"No shit?" Whistling, he said, "Small world. He was a good guy."

"I know."

Brady had seen a lot of things during his fifteen-year tenure as a pilot, but something about the sadness in Stephanie's blue eyes had struck a nerve. When she'd looked at him, calling him by her husband's name, his heart had gone out to her. He'd wanted to go all manly man and charge to her rescue, but that was kind of hard when he was in charge of one hundred and thirty-six souls in addition to hers.

By the book, he shouldn't have left the cockpit. But he'd already been out of his seat and on the way to the forward head when Amanda had called, officially informing him of the situation. Since the flight attendant had added that she thought the woman wasn't so much a threat to others as she was to herself, Brady had figured why not kill two birds with one stone and lend his crew a hand.

"You all right?" Craig asked.

"Sure. Steph couldn't weigh much over a hundred pounds soaking wet."

"I meant, in your head. You look like you've seen a ghost."

Shrugging off his friend's comment, Brady immersed himself in flight duties. Truth was, seeing Stephanie Olmstead again had been a shock. One that disturbed him until they landed.

STEPHANIE WOKE SLOWLY, finding herself covered with a thin, navy blue airline blanket. Beneath the cover, her hands were still zip tied, but thankfully, a quick look around showed her to be on her own in the cabin.

Heavy footsteps sounded on what she assumed was

the jet bridge. Salty-smelling air flared her nostrils. Miami's humidity level was as abrupt of a change from Little Rock as was the rise in temperature.

Her stomach felt as if she'd swallowed a boulder. Dread hanging heavy over the implications of what she'd done.

"This her?" asked a uniformed police officer.

Brady nodded.

"Ma'am," the officer said, "I'm going to have to take you to an airport holding area for questions."

Fat, silent tears slid down her cheeks. "I understand."

Wearing a grim expression, looking as if he wanted to step in, but legally, ethically couldn't, Brady averted his stare.

To him the officer said, "I've taken statements from your crew and the rest of my team is speaking with passengers. Now that she's awake, I'll place Ms. Olmstead in a holding cell and return to the aircraft to debrief you. Ma'am, I'll need you to come with me."

Silently complying, she stood.

Before she could catch it with her restrained hands, the blanket someone had thoughtfully placed over her fell to the floor.

As much as she wished to be rescued, Stephanie knew she'd gotten herself into this mess, and had no one to turn to in escaping the situation but herself. Heart pounding even worse now than it had during her panic attack, she fought for air.

"Ma'am," the officer prompted, motioning her out of her row and into the center aisle.

"W-what about my purse and carry-on?"

"Both are now evidence."

This brought on a fresh wave of nausea.

The airline's space was tight, and on her way out, she brushed against Brady. He, in turn, reached out to steady her. As he had during her panic attack, his kindly touch warmed her. Without saying a word, he told her he cared.

Off the aircraft and standing in the Jetway with the officer alongside her, Stephanie began her walk of shame. In the gate area, police had set up a base of operations, forcing her fellow passengers to stay inside a temporary barricade.

The weight of their stares made her want to hide. If it weren't for her bizarre behavior, they would all be on their way to their final destinations.

"You owe me a gin and tonic, freak." Her former seatmate charged at her, but an officer held him at bay.

Even past the gate, people stared.

Their eyes asked what she'd done to be in cuffs.

The only silver lining in the situation was that she'd chosen to leave the girls at home. If they'd been with her, Lord only knows what might've happened.

Finally, they reached a secure area of Miami International that looked as stark, white and depressing as any interrogation room she'd seen on TV.

"Have a seat," the officer said, directing her to a hard metal chair facing a two-way mirror. Who was behind it? FBI? CIA? As terrified as she'd been on the plane, she was now that afraid of spending the rest of her life in jail. "Need water? Coffee? Something to eat?"

"No, thank you." Judging by her roiling stomach, anything she ate would only sour.

"All right, well, sit tight and my supervisor will be in to question you."

Stephanie could only nod as she awaited her fate.

Chapter Two

"How's it going?" Brady asked one of the last investigators still at the gate. In the four hours since landing, he'd finished postflight paperwork, and though scheduled for a return flight to Memphis, due to the delay brought on by Steph's incident, a floater pilot had gone in Brady's place.

"We're about finished," the tall, thin man said, making a notation on a clipboard. Acne scars marred his complexion, but warm blue eyes and a smile made him the most approachable of the hard-edged security-types. "I just got word that the suspect's story checks out. Looks like your garden-variety crazy."

Brady winced at the guy's cavalier choice in wording. As if Steph's meltdown had been no big deal. Granted, in the grand scheme of things, nothing had happened, but he could only imagine what she was still going through. As Michael's friend, he owed it to the guy to make sure she got through this unscathed.

"So, um—" Brady strove for a casual tone "—what's going to happen to her? The *suspect?*"

The guy shrugged. "Guess she'll go on with her business. Best as I can recall, she's in town to pack up her dead husband's stuff."

"Where is Mrs. Olmstead? Would I be allowed to see her?"

Eyes narrowed, the investigator asked, "Always take this much interest in your passengers?"

"No." And Brady failed to see what business it was of this guy's.

"Whatever. She was a looker. Don't blame you for wanting to tap that."

Blanching at the man's crudeness, Brady asked, "Is she still in the main security area?"

"Far as I know."

"Thanks."

Not in the mood for additional small talk, Brady headed for the Miami Police's airport offices.

Once there, he was pointed to an unwelcoming waiting area that showed years of abuse. Scuffed white walls. Blue vinyl chairs with duct-taped holes. A smell lingering between scalded coffee and BO.

An hour later, he'd finished reading a three-day-old *Miami Herald* and had just started on a tattered *Car Trader* when Stephanie rounded a corner.

"You're here," she said, confusion marring her pretty features. In her left hand, she gripped a sheath of papers. In her right, a flowery quilted purse and a standard black carry-on that caught a ride on the retractable handle of a larger black suitcase with wheels.

Saying what first came to mind, he blurted, "I, ah, thought you'd need help finding your way out of this maze." But getting her safely to the parking lot wasn't the only reason he'd stayed. As for that, the jury was still out. Partially because it was the right thing to do—for Michael. Moreover, because as much as he sensed she needed a friend, so did he.

"Thank you." Her voice was hoarse.

He rose, gesturing for her to start down the long hallway leading to the exit.

Outside, the return to Miami International's usual frenetic pace was jarring. Leaning her luggage against the wall, Stephanie crossed her arms and groaned.

"What's wrong?" he asked. Never had he seen a woman—anyone—appear more fragile. The slump of her shoulders, her waxen complexion, and the redness in her eyes told the story of her horrible day. "I mean, besides the obvious." Hoping to lighten her mood, he added a smile.

Eyes pooling with tears, her lower lip trembled. "I'm so tired, and I'm sure my rental car reservation has been canceled and after all I've just been through, the thought of going to Austin's empty house is killing me." Austin—another mutual friend, let Michael keep a room in the home he'd inherited from his mom. It was in a retirement village and the guys used to give him and Michael crap about leading on the geriatric set. Brady had just gotten an invitation for Austin's wedding, leading him to put two and two together in assuming Steph was in town to pack a few of Michael's things left in Austin's soon-to-be-sold house.

"I don't blame you for dreading that plan."

"You've been great," she said, "especially when I almost took out your plane."

"Not even close," he reasoned.

"Thanks for trying to make me feel better, but if I've learned anything from this situation, it's that I'm not superwoman. When my doctor recommended medication—at least in-flight—I should've taken her up on it."

"Your call. But after the results of your latest trip,

probably a good one." He gave her what he hoped came across as a lighthearted elbow jab.

Resting against the wall alongside her luggage, she closed her eyes. "I've got to get on with things. I don't even know what time it is."

"Five-fifteen Eastern time, but hey, that means it's only a little past three in your usual neck of the woods."

"True." Her faint smile warmed him through and through. He took it as progress in his mission to restore her to what he recalled her usually cheery demeanor.

"Tell you what," he suggested, "how about I help you with the whole rental car drill, and then I'll take you to one of my favorite beachfront restaurants?"

"I don't know…"

"What's to know? Nothing relaxes like a margarita and nachos."

HAVING GIVEN BRADY THE KEYS to the hot-red Sebring convertible he'd talked her into renting, Stephanie arched her head back, letting the sea-scented air wash away the day. Riding alongside Michael's old friend made her feel as if part of her husband was still alive. The sensation was heady. During hours of what she could only call interrogation hell, she'd promised herself that if she ever again saw daylight, she'd work harder at enjoying life, rather than just *living* it.

Michael had been gone nearly a year and a half, but she wasn't. So many times he'd made her promise that should anything ever happen to him, she wouldn't shut down. During hours spent contemplating never seeing her children or friends again, something inside her had come to the realization that shutting down was exactly what she'd done.

"You're awfully quiet over there," her companion said, veering off the freeway and onto a quiet side street.

"Mmm…" Dragging in more greedy gulps of the intoxicating air, she said, "I'd forgotten how amazing it is down here. No wonder Michael flew this route as often as possible."

"Me, too. It's like a minivacation."

The few times Stephanie had been fortunate to snag a standby seat on one of Michael's flights, they'd stayed at Austin's. Though never having had more than a day or two to spend in the sun, they'd made the most of their time, playing on the beach, and after dark, having equally good times in smoky salsa clubs. "Austin's been sweet, letting me put this off as long as I have—packing Michael's things. He offered to do it for me, but I wanted to handle it on my own. You know, as a kind of formality."

He grunted. "I feel for you—never having had the chance to really say goodbye. Yeah. Totally sucks."

Stopped at a red light, she met his stare and then burst out laughing.

"What's funny?"

The light turned green.

"Nothing," she said, laughing so hard she'd started to cry. "All my closest friends have had rambling support speeches, yet you managed to sum up my feelings so s-succinctly." Laughter turned to hot, messy tears that hit from out of nowhere and refused to stop.

Pulling the car into a real-estate office's empty parking lot, Brady turned off the engine, unbuckled his seat belt and hers, and pulled her into his arms.

"Let it out," he urged, rubbing her back, rocking her, soothing her like no one else in her circle had.

Only he wasn't in her circle. She hardly knew him. Yes, in what now seemed like another lifetime, they'd been friends, but she'd spent more time with his wife than him.

Once her sobs had subsided to sniffles, he released her and asked, "Better?"

She nodded.

"Cool." Taking her hand, he smoothed the top. "Then if you agree, I'd like to get a margarita in you before your next meltdown."

THE RESTAURANT WHERE Brady took Stephanie was the antithesis of where she'd spent her afternoon. Gone was the white, and in its place were plaster walls done in vibrant reds, yellows and cobalt-blue. Colorful pots overflowed with trailing ivy and ferns and a half-dozen different types of palms. The tables were covered in mosaic tiles. None of the chairs matched. Open French doors and a live salsa band fueled vibrant pairs of dancers.

Even better, was her dining companion. Brady had long since dressed down his uniform, ditching his jacket, tie and hat and unbuttoning his starched white shirt at the throat. Though she'd spent a lot of time with him over the course of the day, this was the first moment she'd gotten a good look at him. The years they'd been apart had been kind. His face wasn't so much handsome, as it was interesting. A square jaw balanced by a slightly crooked nose. Friendly brown eyes had drawn her in from the start. That afternoon, his hair had been neatly combed. Now, it was a dark, rummaged-through mess that she found infinitely more approachable than what she assumed was his professional look. His best feature was his smile—a little lopsided, but easy with strong white teeth and sincerity that never failed to light his eyes.

"How did you know this outing was exactly what I needed?" Stephanie asked, feeling closer to her husband than she had in a long time. "Michael loved salsa dancing. I bought *him* lessons for his thirtieth birthday."

Laughing, Brady said, "Oh, I know all about it. Me and the guys gave him hell. But it's great that you two had something like that to share. Clarissa and I weren't so lucky."

"The way you say that in the past tense, is she okay?"

He winced. "Depends on how you define it. Like, is she alive and kicking? Yes. Are we still married? No."

"Wow. I'm sorry." Spreading guacamole on a nacho, Stephanie struggled for the right thing to say. She'd always enjoyed Clarissa's company. After Stephanie and Michael moved to Valley View, they lost the close contact with the other couple years ago, but Stephanie had looked forward to reconnecting enough to at least send Christmas cards. "Seems like Michael said you'd had a little girl. Do you see her often?"

"Not nearly as much as I'd like." Downing the last of his margarita, he signaled the waitress for another. "Sometimes I feel like my ex-wife's new husband is trying to take my place."

"That must be rough. I can't imagine not seeing my girls every day. This week without them is going to be long." Snagging another chip, she asked, "Do you mind my asking what happened? You and Clarissa were adorable."

He rubbed his hand along his whisker-stubbled jaw. "Long story short, we grew apart."

"Clarissa started over with a new guy. How about

you?" she asked, munching another guacamole-loaded chip. "Ever think of hooking up with a hottie flight attendant or ticket agent?"

"Nope." He'd answered with such sudden certainty she didn't doubt for a moment that having been burned by love, he wasn't in the market for another romance. "You?"

"Like remarrying?" She laughed. "Of course, I've thought about it—Michael always said that if something should ever happen to him, he didn't want me spending the rest of my life alone. But with two soon-to-be-impressionable girls, it would have to be the real deal."

"You're a tough cookie. I admire your conviction," Brady said.

"But?" Grinning, feeling blessedly loose from the music, good food and even better conversation, she prompted, "I sense we're at odds on this subject."

After a sarcastic snort, he said, "What we have here is not a mere difference of opinion, but more like a polar opposite. Black and white. North and South. You know, total and complete disagreement—but in a respectful way."

"Oh—of course," she said, downing more of her drink.

"I thought I'd found everything I ever wanted only to have Clarissa turn my life into a living hell. No way would I set myself up again for that kind of pain."

"You didn't think the magic of it—love—was worth it?"

He took a minute to ponder this. "Oh—while it lasted, it was amazing. Trouble is, like this delicious meal, it's a treat in the short term. But in the long term, it ends. Badly. You, of all people, should agree."

Brady's words saddened her. His utter lack of faith for the future.

"You've gone quiet," he said. "Did I put my foot in my mouth?"

"No. Just looking for the right words to convey what I'm feeling." Another sip of tequila helped. "Even though what Michael and I shared was cut short, I wouldn't trade it for the world. My memories of him are priceless. Better yet—" She rummaged through her purse for her latest pictures of her girls. Proudly showing him her favorite shots of them covered head to toe in chocolate pudding that'd taken thirty minutes to wash off, she said, "Our love made these two, gorgeous *souvenirs*. I know it must sound corny, but back when you and Clarissa thought each other hung the moon, you made your little girl. Instead of always looking at what went wrong with Clarissa, maybe if every once in a while you pondered what was right, you'd have a different view where dating is concerned."

Expression wry, he asked, "Pollyanna get the memo that you stole her job?"

After sticking out her tongue, she said, "I refuse to apologize for at least trying to stay upbeat. What happened today was a throwback to dark times. When I first heard about Michael, the only thing keeping me alive were our babies growing inside of me. I totally get where you must feel bitter and resentful. But once you get past that, focus on your little girl. Nothing helped me more than being with my twins."

"You have full custody," he argued. "It's understandable that technique worked for you. I see Lola maybe once a month, and even then our visits are strained. I think she'd rather spend the time with her friends instead of with me."

"Boo hoo." Refusing to climb aboard his pity train, she reasoned, "You're a pilot. Gifted with the ability to go anywhere, anytime. I'll bet if you made an effort to see more of your girl, you'd be amazed at the change— not only in her, but yourself."

LONG AFTER BRADY HAD STEPHANIE drop him at his hotel, he had trouble drifting off to sleep. Out of bed, booting up his laptop, he surfed the day's headlines. The panic aboard his flight had made CNN's site. As expected, the incident had been blown entirely out of proportion, featuring comments from only the most disgruntled of all passengers.

As strange as the afternoon had been, the night that had started off on such a high note had also ended sourly. Restless, he stood in front of a sparkling twelfth-floor Miami view and wondered where Stephanie and all of her pie-in-the sky ideals were now? Alone in her dead husband's part-time bed?

After Brady had spent his entire day watching over her, to then be accused of bailing on his relationship with Lola had incensed him. He hadn't so much abandoned his daughter as he had graciously stepped aside, making way for Clarissa's new love, to play the role of Dad. To Brady's way of thinking, his daughter would be far less confused by having just one father in her life rather than two.

Could he have been wrong?

Pacing, he refused to credit Stephanie with more recognition than she'd deserved. Her observations were brought on by exhaustion and tequila. She didn't see his entire picture. The way Clarissa's cheating had messed with his head. He'd thought about returning to Seattle to be closer to Lola. He'd even run the idea by his supervisor, as well as scoping out potential places to live. So what stopped him from taking the plunge?

With a flight in the morning, Brady should've long since been asleep. Too bad fury still had him wired. Knowing he'd no doubt be up for a while, he made a call to his scheduling center.

"WHAT are you doing here?" Stephanie asked Brady at the door of Austin's house. Just past ten in the morning, she wore cut-off jean shorts and one of Michael's ratty old T-shirts. She'd crammed her curls into a scrunchie on top of her head. The PB and J she'd just downed had dribbled purple on the gray fabric between her breasts. "I thought you had a flight?"

"Ever heard of calling in sick?"

Hands on her hips, she cocked her head. "If you love to fly anywhere near as much as Michael, it'd take two broken arms to ground you."

"Busted." Hands jammed in his jean pockets, he said, "Truth? Last night's conversation got to me."

"Which part?" she asked, stepping back while holding open the door to let him in. The day was bright and sunny, meaning it took her eyes a few seconds to adjust to the darker interior. With Austin in Moscow, the curtains were drawn on the usually light-filled space. The kitchen clock's tick seemed unbearably loud. Even though he'd only been gone a few days, the home smelled musty. The peace lily gracing the center of the kitchen table drooped. She made a mental note to water it.

"Everything concerning Lola. Last night, I couldn't rest. I was seriously ticked at you for insinuating that I've abandoned my daughter. But after sleeping on it, I've gotta say you're right. It's somehow easier to avoid the issue than facing it head-on. She's a kid. Of course, she's going to enjoy being around her friends more than me. So I've been choosing the path of least resistance in letting her have her way." Leaning forward, resting his elbows on his knees, now cradling his forehead, he added, "I do feel guilty. Like I'm letting another man raise my kid. I hate it. But no more. Thanks for giving me the kick I needed to make a few tough decisions."

"Like what?" Sitting cross-legged on a tropical-themed sofa, she gestured for him to join her.

He did. "Like, I bitch an awful lot about what I'd like my relationship with Lola to be like, but I haven't done enough to change it. Drumroll, please..." Rolling a beat on his thighs, he announced, "It'll be rough at first, but I'm moving to Seattle."

"Just like that?"

Nodding, he said, "It's actually been a long time coming. I've checked out apartments and everything. I just—" He grinned her way. "I needed an old friend to remind me about what's important. And my kid—she's *el numero uno*."

"I'm happy for you." Stephanie leaned over for a quick, heartfelt hug, then asked, "When are you taking the plunge?"

"Overall, I'm probably looking at a month or two for everything to be finalized—you know, with my flight routes changed. I asked for the week off, and tomorrow I'll get the ball rolling."

"And today?" she asked, her pulse curiously racing in anticipation of his answer.

"Today, I hope you'll let me repay you."

"For what? If anything, I owe you for what happened yesterday."

"Assuming we can agree to disagree—" his grin managed to be lopsided, yet adorable "—let's ditch this boring old house and go to the beach."

Chapter Three

"Better?" Brady asked Stephanie from the white chaise longue alongside her. They shared a beachfront umbrella on the glistening turquoise shore. One of the perks of being a pilot was having friends in great places. Like Pete Danvers, whose sixteenth-floor condo included access to this pristine stretch of shore. Like Austin, Pete flew international routes and was rarely home to enjoy the fruits of his labor. A breeze helped with the humidity, carrying with it the sound of seagulls and the scent of someone's grilled lunch.

"You have no idea how much better…" Covering a yawn, she said, "I didn't know how awful packing up Michael's things was going to be."

"Have much more to go?"

"Unfortunately, yeah. My hubby was a horrible pack rat. Sentimental to a fault, he kept everything from ticket stubs to museum brochures."

Rolling to face her, Brady asked, "Tossing it all?"

"No." Her lone word carried extra oomph. Implying he was an ass for even suggesting such a thing. "I plan to make scrapbooks commemorating his life. Dozens if that's what it takes to keep all of the things he held dear."

Animated, Stephanie's abundance of corkscrew curls

rode the wind, resembling a seriously cute mane. Her pink one-piece with a ruffled bust managed being both sexy and demure. "Ever consider the fact that by spending so much time in the past, you're doing the exact opposite of what Michael specifically told you to do?" Sitting up, he planted one foot in the warm sand. "Don't get me wrong, Michael was a great guy, but think about it. He told you to get a life, but here you are, planning out a task that's going to take years to complete."

Scrunching her pretty features, she argued, "It won't take anywhere near that long. And, anyway, what do you care?"

Good question. Maybe because all of this heat and sun-shot water were making him want to stop talking about Stephanie's dead husband, and start getting on with the more fun portions of their day.

Jumping to his feet, he shouted, "Last one in the water has to clean Austin's nasty grout!"

"You noticed that, too?" Steph took the time to ask. Precious time, since he was already halfway to the waves.

"Cheat!" Chasing after him, she was definitely last. "How did you even see Austin's grout?"

"Lucky guess," he admitted. "Last time I was at his house—like over a year ago, it needed work then."

"You know what this means, don't you?"

Eyebrows raised, he asked, "You'll need to pick up bleach and rubber gloves on the way home?"

With a grin and wicked sparkle to her eyes, Steph landed a well-aimed shove to his chest. Too bad for her, he wasn't going down without taking her with him.

Laughing and sputtering water, she crashed against his chest while his back hit the sandy bottom. A rogue wave body-slammed both of them.

"You're horrible!" she said, still laughing and clinging to him for balance. She felt amazing against him.
Curvy. Wet. Hot.

On autopilot, he did what any sane guy would and
kissed her. Hands loose on her hips, warm water swirling at his feet, he tilted his head to get better access,
which she granted. She tasted sweet—forbidden. Her
breathy moans only made him want her more.

Drawing back, expression dazed, she put her hands to
her lips. "Oh, no..." Awareness of what they'd just done
brightened her eyes and she looked almost as panicked
as she had on the plane.

He struggled to remain calm. "Sorry. I don't know
what came over me. It won't happen again."

She shook her head, took a deep breath, then nodded.
"I'm sorry, too."

For an awkward few moments, they stood in foam-
ing surf. A few dozen yards down the beach, little kids
fought over a Frisbee. Their voices were jarring, reminding him where he was. Who he was with. A good
friend's wife.

Hooking her thumb toward their belongings, she said,
"I should probably get back to Austin's."

"Yeah." He cleared his throat. "With the move and
all, I've got stuff to do, too."

Given different circumstances, he might've offered
to help her. Now, he felt as if in kissing her, he'd abused
the privilege of being her friend.

The dripping return trip to their gear wasn't near as
much fun as their running into the surf. Instead of feeling soft on the soles of his feet, the sand now itched. The
once healing sun was bringing on a burn. Once salty air
suddenly stank like dead fish.

"I am sorry." He drew his white T-shirt over his head.

"It wasn't a big deal," she said with an obviously forced smile. Having crammed her towel, paperback and lotion into her jumbo beach bag, she put on a pink cover-up and grabbed white flip-flops. "Ready?"

And then some.

On a scale of one to ten on the Brady Screwup Meter, kissing Stephanie had spiked him off the chart.

BACK AT AUSTIN'S, WHERE BRADY had left his rental car, *awkward* didn't do their mutual silence justice. He'd never been big on knowing the right thing to say, and this time was no exception. "Guess I should get going, huh?"

She nodded too vigorously for his already decimated ego. "That'd probably be best."

"Why do I get the feeling you're ticked off?" Moreover, why couldn't he leave well enough alone and simply get behind the wheel and drive?

Sighing, she said, "I'm not angry, Brady, just hurt and confused—not only by your actions, but my own. What happened? I don't kiss random strangers, and—"

"Stop. The thing is we're hardly strangers. We used to hang out all the time. What happened at the beach is the result of two lonely people losing themselves in a moment." Hand beneath her chin, he asked, "How long has it been since you've had fun like that? Laughing and playing like when you were a kid?"

"A while. But that doesn't make it better. Clarissa's my friend. I still can't get used to the idea that you don't *belong* to her."

"Just like you still *belong* to Michael?"

"This conversation is stupid. Going in circles. It was wonderful seeing you again, but let's leave it at that."

His chest tight, he said, "Agreed."

She extended her hand for him to shake. "Thanks again for your help on the plane. You were a godsend."

Wishing he could've done more, he enfolded her hand in his. "It was my pleasure. But speaking of airplanes, you okay for your trip home? Need me to arrange for you to have an escort?"

"I appreciate the thought, but not necessary." Releasing his hand, she folded her arms. Standing beneath a shady patch provided by trellised bougainvillea, she said, "I'm a big girl, Brady. A capable businesswoman and mom. The last thing I need is a sitter."

Clearing his throat, he said, "That may well be, and I hate pointing out the obvious, but if you pull another stunt like that last one on an airline, you're not likely to get off so easy."

"You think the hell those men put me through was *easy?* They asked everything from whether or not I was suicidal to if I had a mental illness. I'm a widowed mother of two infants. A five-foot-nothing pastry chef from Valley View, Arkansas. Why in the world would they think me capable of taking hostages?"

Standing behind her, trying to be as gentle as possible, he cupped his hands to her shoulders. "Maybe because in your, ah, panicked condition, I had to zip tie your hands to keep from you hurting yourself or others."

"You told me there was no way I could've opened that cabin door."

"True." He kneaded the knots between her shoulder blades. "But what if you'd gone nuts in the galley, and smashed all of the pretzels? And the stout gentleman who'd been sitting beside you would've not only lost his gin and tonic, but his snack? Now that might've caused a complete meltdown of our airline society." Turning her to face him, he said, "God's honest truth, Steph, you have no business flying alone. Even with medication, you need help."

"I'll be fine."

"Then I guess I should get going."

"Probably." Did she have to be so agreeable? As though his leaving was the best news she'd heard all day? "Oh—" She headed for the house's front door, inserting Michael's key into the lock. "Before I forget, I've got something for you." She'd already gone inside without inviting him to follow.

He rammed his hands in the pockets of his swim trunks, waiting, waiting, feeling like an idiot just standing in the hot sun.

A few minutes later, the door creaked open, and Stephanie handed him a plastic baggie filled with photos. "I found these, and thought you might like to have them."

"Thanks," he said, already flipping through the pile. There were a few of him and Michael playing B-ball on a layover in Chicago. It'd taken an hour's walk from their hotel to find a court. Another pilot had come along for the exercise, snapping the shot. Others featured Michael, Brady and mutual friends in various not-so-professional poses in bars all over the world. Until now, slammed with reminders of just how close he and Michael had once been, Brady hadn't truly faced the finality of his friend being gone.

"Okay, then…" Putting the photos back in the bag, he struggled for something to say. Throat tight, he finally settled on "Do we want to exchange phone numbers?"

"I don't think so. What would be the point?"

Damn, but she knew how to use words as a weapon. Her refusal to give him her number sliced through him.

"Agreed," he said, more to save face than because he thought she'd made the slightest bit of sense. "So this is it? We say our goodbyes and that'll be that?"

"You expected more?" she asked, eyebrows raised.

Had he? And if so, what? Another kiss? Crazy. As was the unease stemming from the thought of never seeing her again.

"Need anything for your trek back to your hotel? Austin has sodas in his fridge."

"I'm good," he said.

"All right, then…" She enveloped him in a hug. She felt so small and fragile in his arms that he wanted to scoop her up and carry her away. He wanted to make everything better and guarantee her every day had plenty of smiles. "Thank you. I'll never forget your kindness."

"Ditto." After kissing the top of her head, he stepped back, drinking in one long, last look. Memorizing the freckles dotting her nose. Her big, blue eyes and crazy hair that she never quite tamed. "Promise to take your medicine before flying?"

She grinned despite looking on the verge of more tears and made an exaggerated X across her chest.

"This is boring."

A few days later, in the living area of what would hopefully be his new Seattle home, Brady frowned at his daughter. To the condo's rental agent, he asked, "Is there a furnished, all-utilities-included option?"

"Of course." The squinty-eyed woman shoved a folder in his face. "We offer gas, electric, water and cable. For furniture and accessories, we have three styles to choose from. Contemporary, French Provincial or country.

You'll need to decide a week before your anticipated arrival."

"I like the French stuff," Lola said. "Get that, Dad."

"French it is." Brady couldn't care less what his sofa and tables looked like, but if Lola did, then he'd do whatever it took to make her happy.

The agent made a note on the paperwork he'd already started filling out. "As for your cable, would you like basic or expanded with premium channels?"

"HBO! HBO!"

"Basic will be fine," Brady said, knowing Clarissa would have his hide if he let Lola watch more than her allotted hour a day.

"You never let me have what *I* want," Lola said. "Why do you have to always side with Mom?"

"She's precious." The agent's thin-lipped smile told a different story. She'd placed a pile of forms on the granite kitchen counter. "Now, if you'd initial here and here, and then sign the lines I've flagged, all that's left is a check."

Jaw clenched, Brady signed the document promising to reside in the condo for the next year.

"*Dad-dy,*" his precious child whined. "This is *soooo* boring. You promised this wouldn't take long, and then we'd do something fun."

"Oh, we're going to have a great time," he assured her, handing the agent her forms. "You'll have the unit ready by the first of next week?"

Nodding, the woman's sleek black bob was as motionless as her expression. "When you get into town, just drop by the clubhouse for your keys."

Behind the wheel of his silver rental sedan, Brady

asked his daughter, "What's wrong with you? Acting like such a brat when I'm moving here for you."

"No, you're not," she said, lifting her chin. "You're moving to Seattle because you feel guilty about not spending enough time with me. Mom told me so."

Brady counted to five in his head—he couldn't have held his words for a full count of ten. "First, I'm sorry for what I just said. It came out wrong. I'm not back in Seattle for you, but for us both. Somewhere along the line, you seem to have forgotten that I'm your dad."

She rolled her eyes.

"It's stunts like that I'm talking about, Lola. Whether you like me, or not, you will respect me. My meeting with the rental agent was important to me. How would you feel if the next time you have a gymnastics game, I mouthed off in front of your coach and friends?"

"That's different. And, anyway, you don't even go to half of my *meets*." With a put-upon huff, she crossed her arms.

"Now that I'm back in town, plan on seeing a whole lot more of me."

"Great. Like having Uncle Vince around all the time isn't embarrassing enough? Now, I have to have two dads?"

"I was the only father in the delivery room when you were born. I was the guy changing your diapers and wiping your nose for the first four years of your life. That gives you only one dad—me."

Pouting, she said, "Geez, Mr. McGuire, take a pill."

"You didn't have to come all this way to babysit," Stephanie complained. She sat on the foot of Michael's bed, surrounded by his things, which she still hadn't finished sorting despite having been in Miami for almost a week.

Her identical twin sister picked up one of Michael's memorabilia boxes, flipping through snapshots of happier times. "I prefer to think of myself more as a seriously high-paid nanny."

"I'm not paying you a dime," Stephanie said. "Like I told you over the phone, I'm perfectly capable of getting back to Arkansas all on my own."

"Just like you thought getting to Miami was going to be no biggie?" Setting down the box, Lisa slipped her arm around Stephanie's shoulders. "For heaven's sake, your panic attack was so epic you ended up on CNN. Doesn't that kind of scream 'I need help' to you?"

Up from the bed, Stephanie took one of Michael's sweatshirts, burying her face in it, desperate for a trace of his smell. How had a simple trip to pack a few boxes gotten so out of control? Her emotions were chaotic at best. Mostly just catastrophic. "I've got bigger problems than flying," Stephanie confessed.

"Oh, honey. Are you still dealing with grief? If so, I've got numbers of counselors who—"

Stephanie tossed Michael's sweatshirt on top of the dresser, then covered her face with her hands, vehemently shaking her head. "This has nothing to do with Michael."

"Then what?" Kicking off floral sneakers, Lisa sat cross-legged on the bed.

"I kissed a man."

Eyes wide, Lisa asked, "Who?"

Stephanie groaned. "Remember that nice couple we used to live next door to in Dallas? Clarissa and Brady?"

"Yeah…"

"Well, Brady was the pilot on my flight. I saw him in his uniform and in my less-than-stable condition, thought he was Michael. He was so kind, even waited at the airport security office for me. He took me out to dinner and we laughed and enjoyed a delicious meal. He told me that he and Clarissa were divorced. The next day, we went to the beach and we were soaking in the sun and running through the waves and—" Hand over her mouth, she mumbled, "I'm not sure if I kissed him, or he kissed me, but at the time, it felt so natural, but then—"

"Time-out," Lisa said, crossing her hands into a T. "First things first, did you like it? Kissing him?"

"Well…yes, but that's not the point."

"What is? Why are you flipping out over a kiss?"

Pacing, Stephanie said, "I'm flipping out because I very much not only liked the kiss, but being with Brady. I liked everything about him. He's compassionate and funny and when he laughs, it's like his whole body lights up, and—"

"Breathe." Blocking Stephanie's path, her sister said, "When Michael died, I was so scared for you. Still am. But since when is kissing a great guy problematic? Steph, I know Michael and I didn't always see eye to eye, but one thing we both agreed on was that if anything should ever happen to him that you go on with your life. It's been over a year that he's been gone. Why are you being so hard on yourself?"

Hands back over her face, Stephanie squealed.

"Now, what's wrong?"

"You said *hard,* and during the kiss, well…" Hands lowered, her cheeks blazed. "What's wrong with me? I never think dirty things like that."

"Ask me," Lisa said, fanning herself with a 2007 Super Bowl program, "it's about damned time."

Chapter Four

"See?" Lisa said once their flight safely landed in Little Rock, "With me by your side, that wasn't so bad, was it?"

"Not at all," Steph admitted while they taxied to the gate. "But then my medicine makes me feel like I'm flying without the benefit of a plane. Does that nullify my accomplishment?"

Gathering their two magazines and a bottled water from her seat pocket, Lisa asked, "Would you rather be high or back in a padded cell?"

"It wasn't padded. In fact, there wasn't a single soft item to be found."

Sighing, Lisa rolled her eyes. "I rest my case."

With her twin's arrival, the rest of Steph's week in Miami had passed in a busy blur.

They'd given most of Michael's clothes and ragtag furniture to charity. For his mementos, Steph had arranged for the boxes to be shipped to Valley View.

Being with Brady felt like a dream.

"You excited to see the twins?" her sister asked.

Throat unexpectedly tight, Steph nodded.

Lisa took her hand. "You're going to be okay, you know? Great, even."

She and her sister had always had a knack for sensing

each other's moods. Never had she been happier to have someone in her life who knew her inside and out. "I love you."

"Ditto."

While the plane jerked to a stop and a flight attendant opened the cabin door, Steph and her twin shared a quick hug.

It took five minutes for the passengers in front of them to file off the plane. It took another five to walk the long concourse to where friends and family gathered to pick up arriving travelers. When Stephanie first caught sight of Tag and Olivia holding her smiling, waving babies, happy tears stung her eyes. Emotionally, the past week could only be described in terms of a battle. One from which she'd just now emerged victorious.

Running, she laughed through tears. "You're both so adorable," she crooned, kissing Melanie and then Michaela.

"Thanks," Tag quipped. "I wasn't sure about my hair, but I guess it looks good after all."

Olivia gave him a jab. "Welcome home," she said, passing Steph Michaela, who had been her firstborn, and was named in honor of her father. She'd dressed the girls in matching pink corduroys paired with pricey-looking cashmere sweaters as soft as the girls' blond curls.

After taking Michaela into her arms, drinking in her sweet, familiar scent of lotion and baby shampoo, Stephanie reached for Melanie.

"Steph," her sister warned. "Remember what your doctor said about holding both girls at once. You're going to inflame your bursitis."

"I don't care," Stephanie said, "that's why the Good Lord invented ibuprofen."

Olivia and Tag laughed, but Lisa didn't.

She worried too much. Ever since Michael's passing, she'd appointed herself Steph's watchdog. Whether it be on matters of child care, house maintenance or health, Lisa was always on hand to remind Stephanie just how tenuous of a situation she was in. As a single mom of two, she didn't have the luxury of being achy or sick. She had too much to do, which Lisa was usually happy to point out. While they'd been in Miami, her sister had been the old Lisa. Fun and supportive again as opposed to nagging.

"Don't ruin this for me," Stephanie whispered to her twin while Tag and Olivia fussed over Flynn, who had just pitched his favorite pink hippo from his stroller and was now screaming about it. "All I could think of during this hellish week was getting my arms back around these two."

"I understand," Lisa said, "but that doesn't mean you should ignore your doctor's advice. Look what good that did you on your Dallas-to-Miami flight."

Trying to change the subject, Steph asked Olivia, "How much do I owe you for the girls' posh new outfits? They're gorgeous."

Olivia waved off her question. "Don't even think of giving me money for what amounted to an afternoon's entertainment for Flynn and I. We love shopping, and it was a hoot finally getting to pick out girly stuff."

"Sure?" Steph asked, easing Michaela into the front of the twins' double stroller, and then Melanie into the back.

"Absolutely. Need help?" Olivia asked, hovering nearly as bad as Lisa. Outside of her sister, Stephanie hadn't told a soul about her high-altitude meltdown, which meant, judging by her concerned expression, her friend must've heard about it on her own.

"No, thanks. I'm good." Rising, careful not to favor her suddenly aching back, chest and forearms, she gave her friend a hug. "That was sweet of you to get my girls a new winter outfit. I wasn't prepared for the cold."

"Seriously," Olivia reassured, "it was our pleasure."

"I hate breaking up this hug fest," Tag said, "but we're about to get run over."

Stephanie looked up to see that while she'd enjoyed her reunion, a new crowd had moved in. Some waved Welcome Home banners, and others had American flags.

A glance down the concourse from where they'd just come showed a trio of desert camo-wearing, smiling soldiers. Returning home from Iraq?

Hastily looking away, she busied herself with gathering her carry-on and then pushing the twins' stroller toward the baggage-claim area.

She hadn't missed Lisa's latest worried look, or the way Olivia swatted Tag.

He mouthed *sorry.*

Stephanie wanted to crawl inside one of the suitcases rounding the carousel. Her friends must think she was a total basket case. Yes, seeing other women laughing through tears while crushing their soldiers in reunion embraces was agonizing, but Stephanie didn't begrudge them their happiness. Of course, she still hurt, but she was a big girl. She'd long ago learned life wasn't the least bit fair.

Once all of the luggage had been gathered, the ride home in Tag's Hummer was awkward and long. The Razorbacks had played that afternoon at War Memorial Stadium, meaning traffic from the airport to Valley View was a nightmare. With three babies in car seats, Lisa and Stephanie and their luggage were squeezed in. Luckily, Olivia and Lisa kept up a steady stream of chatter while Tag kept his focus on the road.

After dropping off Lisa, the trip to Steph's three-bedroom ranch house was short.

Too bad unloading her suitcase, carry-on and all of Michaela and Melanie's gear took considerably longer. The sky was gray and wind brisk. Tag offered to do all of the hauling but while Olivia stayed with the babies, Stephanie helped pile everything in the entry hall, figuring she'd sort it later.

The house was in a newish subdivision, and without benefit of trees, the cold sliced through her. After Miami's lushness, seeing her dreary home did little to brighten her mood. She and Michael had had big plans for the place. But with him gone, landscaping and her dream of painting the house a cheerful yellow had been indefinitely put on hold.

At the airport, she'd been so happy to see the girls. Now that the initial euphoria had worn off, exhaustion took its toll.

"You going to be all right?" Olivia asked once everything was in the house—including the twins, who were busy reacquainting themselves with the toys in their playpen. Flynn was asleep in his car seat.

"I'm fine," Steph assured.

"I almost forgot," Olivia said, jogging to the car. From beneath the front seat, she took a casserole dish. "I made you enchiladas for dinner. I know how much you like them, and thought you might be too tired to cook."

Warmed by her friend's thoughtfulness, Stephanie accepted the dish and tried not to cry. "Th-thank you."

"You're so welcome." Expression clouded with worry, Olivia said, "I wish we didn't live so far away."

"Quit," Steph scolded. "You're starting to sound like Lisa. Even before Michael's passing, I learned to be self-sufficient."

"Is your heater good to go?" Tag asked, hunching with his hands in his pockets and back to the wind. "It's supposed to drop to the twenties tonight."

"Yes, *Dad*," Steph said with a forced smile. "I had it checked during the first sign of a cold snap."

"Don't get sassy with me," he teased. "You're not too old for a spanking."

Olivia conked the back of his head. "On that note, I'm getting you out of here." To Steph, she said, "Love you. Call if you need anything."

"I will," Stephanie promised, even though for pride's sake, she probably wouldn't.

Holding the casserole with one hand, she waved with her other, struggling to swallow the lump in her throat as her friends drove away.

HOURS LATER, WITH THE TWINS bathed and fed and tucked into their cribs, Stephanie stood at the kitchen window, staring out at the dark.

Wind rattled the glass, and a light drizzle made the cold feel as if it were seeping into her bones. It was only eight, yet it felt more like midnight. She was just summoning the energy to nuke some of Olivia's enchiladas when the phone rang.

Lisa.

Skipping the usual pleasantries, Stephanie asked, "What did I do now that you need to nag about?"

"Actually," her twin said, "I'm calling to apologize. I didn't mean to come off like a bitch at the airport."

"Then why did you?" Stephanie took the glass enchilada pan from the fridge, and scooped a portion into a bowl.

After a long pause, Lisa said, "I was jealous."

"Huh?" Her meal in the microwave for two minutes, Steph sat at the kitchen table. Now that she thought about it, Lisa's voice sounded raspy. "Have you been crying?"

"A-and drinking wine," she said with a sniffle. "At the airport, I wanted what you have. People to actually come home to. My turtle, George, doesn't count."

"Oh, Lisa, of course he counts. I'm sure in his own way, George really loves you."

The microwave beeped.

"N-not the way the girls love you. You should've seen their little eyes light up. I know you lost Michael too soon but he totally loved you. And then you meet up with a guy you hardly even know and get great kisses. What am I doing wrong that I can't be more like you?"

Laughing, ignoring her still-beeping meal, Steph asked, "Why would you even want to be like me? I'm a walking disaster. CNN did a cover story on my lack-luster hijacking techniques."

"They did not," her twin argued. "It was hardly even a blurb."

"Well, it was my blurb, and I'm still mortified."

"About the panic attack," she probed, "or the kiss?"

Cringing through a giggle, she admitted, "Both. Worse yet, ever since the kiss, I've wanted to see him again."

"So? Call him?"

"First, I'd have to stalk him by finding his number."

"Checked your e-mail since you've been home?"

"No…why?"

Through another sniffle, Lisa said, "He was ridiculously easy to track down. Call him, Steph. Now. Second chances don't come all that often. I-If this is your cosmic do-over, you should seize it."

"Sweetie, put down the wine and get over here—no, scratch that. You shouldn't be driving. What you should do is fix yourself a nice bowl of soup, and then go to sleep."

Crying anew, Lisa said, "I'm tired of being lonely."

"Me, too. But that's why we have each other. So we don't have to be alone. And my girls are yours, too. We're a family."

"I—I know. I'm sorry I even called. I j-just wanted you to know that I think you should call him."

Finally answering the microwave's beep, Stephanie said, "Who knows? Maybe I will."

"DAD?"

"Yes, hon?" Brady looked up from the Sunday *Seattle Times* to find his little girl standing in the hall leading to her room, hands on her hips.

"I don't have enough closet space."

"And…" Lola was eight! What the hell was Clarissa teaching her?

"Can I put some of my clothes in your room?"

"I suppose, but you only brought one suitcase for the weekend. How much stuff did you cram in?"

Rolling her eyes, she said, "Geez, Dad, do you have to be all up in my *bizness?*"

"Carry on." Once she'd left, he returned to the story he'd been reading on the state's unpreparedness for another major oil spill. Great. Like he didn't already have enough to worry about in how he was going to entertain Lola that afternoon.

"Dad!" she shouted from his room. Her voice sounded muffled, leading him to assume she was still in his closet. "Who are all of these people?"

Sighing, he put down his paper. "What people?"

She wandered into the living room with the plastic bag filled with photos that Stephanie had given him. Never one for open sentimentality, he'd stashed them on a top shelf. "Who's this lady with Mom?"

Stephanie. Younger, and without the sorrow on her face that he'd seen in Miami. She and his former wife sat on top of a picnic table, hamming for the camera, making bunny faces. "An old friend."

"How come I've never seen all of these before?"

"Long story."

"I'm not a baby," she reminded, snuggling on the sofa alongside him.

"Okay... Before you were born, your mom and I used to be neighbors with this woman and her husband. Before moving here, I was in Miami and ran into her. She gave me the pictures."

"Does Mom know?"

He shook his head.

"Mom looks really pretty here. I like her hair long." She ran a finger over her mother's form.

"Me, too."

"If she grew her hair out again, would you two get back together?"

If only it were that simple.

"I mean, I like Uncle Vince, and all, but you're cuter."

That knowledge brought a small measure of comfort. "No, hon. Me and your mom are done."

"Do you date anyone?"

"Where did that come from?"

She shrugged. "I heard mom talking about it with Grandma. She said you're never going to get over her because you won't date anyone else."

Ouch. "Wanna get out of here? Maybe head for the zoo?"

"Yeah, but her saying that made me mad. I think you're cute, and if you're not with Mom, you should totally hook up with someone else."

Hook up? Where the hell was his little girl learning this stuff? Brady sighed, suddenly feeling old.

Chapter Five

"What are you doing?" Stephanie asked her sister over the phone Sunday night. After spending the afternoon playing with Tag and Olivia's baby, Flynn, the girls had conked out early.

"Just painting my nails. Why?"

"Come over right away. You have to hear this crazy message on my machine."

Sighing, or maybe just blowing on her nails, Lisa whined, "Do I have to? It's like seriously freakin' cold outside. Can't you just play it for me now?"

"No, and yes, you have to come now or I'll tell Mom how bad you were on your cruise."

"You wouldn't?"

Twenty minutes later, Lisa hobbled through the front door with purple toe dividers laced onto her bare feet.

Shivering, she said, "So let's hear it. I still have to put on a mud mask."

In the kitchen, Steph hit the play button on her answering machine. In a seriously faked man's voice someone said, "Yo, Steph! *Waz* up? This is Brady McGuire and I wanted you to know I'm available for a hot date! Call me!"

A second message featured the same imposter, only with a little girl's giggle in the background. "Hey, it's me again! I forgot to give you my number." After leaving cell, home and work contact info, the caller finished with more muffled giggles. "I know you really want to date me, so call!"

Scrunching her nose, Lisa said, "Please tell me that wasn't really him?"

"No, thank goodness."

"There is one obvious solution to this dilemma." Lisa shuffled to the kitchen table. She pulled out a chair and sat, then leaned over to blow on her toes. "Call him."

"But—"

"No buts. Since you dragged me over here, the least you can do is call the guy. Now I gotta go. I have a date with that mud pack."

After her twin left, Stephanie once again found herself alone with the phone. Finally, curiosity won over sanity.

It took five rings before Brady picked up.

"Hello?" The rich baritone of his voice made the butterflies in her stomach go crazy.

"Um, hey. It's me, Stephanie Olmstead. I got these strange messages, claiming they were from you, only—"

Groaning, he asked, "Did the caller happen to sound like an eight-year-old girl going on thirty pretending to be a fortysomething man?"

Stephanie laughed. "As a matter of fact…"

"I'm so sorry. But this explains Lola's behavior." After relaying an embarrassing exchange he and his daughter had over her old photo, he asked, "I'm not sure whether to be proud of her detective skills, or mortified by her penchant for impersonation."

"No harm done," Steph said, relieved he hadn't been the caller, yet in the same breath saddened by the bigger issue—that Brady sounded as if he hadn't wanted to be the caller. Her sister's voice in her head, urging her along, Stephanie fussed with a stray curl. "I guess I kind of regretted how we left things in Miami."

He laughed. "Likewise. I've found myself thinking of you. Wondering how you're getting along."

Remembered white-hot Miami sun warmed her through and through. "I'm good. You?"

"A month and a half later, I'm finally living in Seattle. The logistics were a nightmare, but now I've found a routine."

"That's wonderful. What does Lola think of this development?"

"Verdict's still out." His chuckle was akin to winning a prize. "We have a love/hate thing going, but I can't tell you how good it feels being back in her daily life."

"I'm proud of you," she said, hoping her admission didn't come off as condescending. "I can't imagine how hard it must be seeing Clarissa and her new husband again, but I'll bet you and Lola will be closer in no time."

"Let's just hope that in the process, she doesn't get any more bright ideas about appointing herself my social director."

"Really," she assured, "this sort of thing happens all the time."

"Uh-huh."

His laugh calmed her nerves. "Okay, truth? Last thing I expected was hearing from your daughter, but now that we've talked...I'm glad."

"Me, too."

After a few minutes of catching up, him describing his new apartment, her delivering a play-by-play of

her twins' commando crawling techniques, there was
a longish pause.

And then Brady said, "This is probably going to
sound out there, but I'm taking Lola and four of her
friends to some teen heartthrob's concert at Key Arena
this weekend. Want to help me chaperone? Assuming
you could land a babysitter."

"In Seattle?" Was he out of his ever-loving mind?

"Yeah, but I have my own plane. I'll pick you up.
Talking you through the flight process might make it
easier. Michael loved flying. I know he'd hate for you
to now be afraid."

"He would be upset with me over the way I freaked
out…" Erratic thoughts, fluctuating between terror, her
responsibilities to her babies and finally school-girl
excitement, Stephanie gushed, "Oh, what the heck?
I'll make arrangements for the twins to stay with my
friends. I can't believe I'm agreeing to this!" She put a
hand to her flushed cheek.

Brady had his own plane, and would travel all that
way? Just for her? Pulse supersonic, she tried to focus
more on the prospect of conquering her fear of flying,
rather than the vision of their surf-flavored kiss. She
didn't want something like that to happen again. Michael
might've been all for her starting over, but if her reaction
to Brady's impromptu advances had taught her anything,
it's that she wasn't anywhere near ready to put her heart
out on the line again.

The next morning, Stephanie pressed a copper turkey
cookie cutter into fragrant sugar-cookie dough. Repeat-
ing the action a dozen times, she placed the birds on a
sheet pan, pleased with the result.

The bell jingled over the front door, signaling she
had a customer. Marching out of the back, Stephanie

was happy to see one of her favorite customers, Paula Fletcher.

"Hear you're off on a big date." The woman's red wig resembled a poorly trimmed shrub and her glasses had enough bling to blind were she to stand in the sun.

"I hardly call it a date. More like an outing." Stephanie retrieved the woman's special-order cornucopia cookies she'd wanted for her grandkids, and then rang her up. "Where'd you hear about it?"

"Ran into your sister at the bank." Paula removed a bedazzled pink wallet from her purse. "She told me you and Michael used to be *couple* friends with Brady and his ex. I like that. Makes me feel better about you flying off with him. Although all of us down at the beauty shop are worried you might not have properly checked his credentials."

Cringing inside, Stephanie became highly concerned about the state of her untidy napkins.

"Lucky for you," Paula rambled on, "a client of mine has a plane down at the municipal airport, and she said, her husband did a little checking, and your Brady has a plane that costs more than half the houses in this town. In fact—"

"Paula." Stephanie struggled for just the right way to tell her valued customer to mind her own business! "Brady's hardly *mine,* and while I appreciate you looking out for me, really, I've got this whole thing covered."

Looking unconvinced, Paula harrumphed. "If you say so. Just be sure to take your medicine. We don't want another Miami incident on our hands."

Swell. Was there any part of her life off-limits from the whole town?

Thankfully, another customer came to the rescue by needing her amaretto éclair order stat. Usually, her friend and employee, Helen, ran the front of the shop, but she'd taken an early lunch, so that when Brady arrived, Stephanie would be free to leave.

An hour passed, during which Stephanie helped more customers while every so often popping into the kitchen to check on cookies and the batch of cherry turnovers she'd just started. Brady had said he'd be in around eleven. Meaning, he was due in just under twenty minutes.

Butterflies didn't do justice to the riot in her stomach. More like attacking locusts!

Even though she should've been rolling out turnovers, she made a hasty call to check up on her girls. Michaela had been extra fussy. They attended the same Montessori day care as Olivia's son. Some months, it was a struggle to afford, but while working, she needed to know her girls were receiving expert care. Olivia had offered to pick up all three infants, keeping them with her over the weekend.

The bell over the door jingled six more times before she looked up from the front counter to see Brady.

Hand to her runaway heart, it took a moment to find her composure. Though his eyes were hidden behind dark Oakley sunglasses and his cheeks ruddy from November wind and sun, when he aimed his strong white smile at her, his rakish charm drew her in anew.

Chapter Six

"Hey…" He slipped off his glasses, tucking them in an interior pocket of a weathered leather coat.

Not thinking, just doing, she ran out from behind the counter to crush him in a hug. He made her feel closer to Michael. Like in reuniting with one of his friends, a piece of her husband was still with her. "I missed you."

Laughing, he returned her hug full-force and said, "I missed you, too. You look beautiful."

Stepping back, putting her hand to her no doubt flour-smudged hair, she turned away to hide flaming cheeks. "You need corrective lenses. But thanks."

"You're welcome." Looking at his surroundings, he whistled. "Impressive. You did all of this?"

Humbled by his praise, she said, "Michael and my sister helped. The three-story building had been condemned, and we bought it for owed taxes. It took six months and more cash than I like to remember to get it to this state." The redbrick, former general store had been built in 1903. After thirty years of its intended use, the corner building sat vacant during the Great Depression. Since then, it'd been used as everything from a day care to a law firm. Water damage decimated the upper floors. Downstairs, all that remained of the original finishes were the high, pressed-tin ceiling and lovingly restored maple floors.

From there, they'd painted the walls a sunny yellow and varnished the maple trim. At an auction, they'd found an antique, marble-topped counter. On top of it sat an old brass cash register. Behind the counter were the custom glass cases where her pastries were stored. Since the industrial kitchen had taken up most of the first floor, there had only been room for three tables, but they were also antique—round oak glowing with lemon oil. Wing chairs were upholstered in a rich burgundy-and-honey floral brocade. French country plaid curtains framed tall, paned windows. Finishing out the decor was Stephanie's rooster collection and vases filled year-round with fresh flowers.

"Hungry?" she asked from behind the counter, gesturing toward an assortment of fresh-baked treats.

"You know it. I'll have a cinnamon roll and black coffee."

"Excellent choice." Glad for the diversion of filling his order, she took his roll from the case, setting it on a saucer before filling a mug from a brass and copper coffee urn that was from the 1800s.

"How much do I owe you?"

She waved off his offer. "How was your flight?"

"Uneventful. You weren't on it." He winked.

"Ha-ha." It was nice to laugh over the incident.

Lisa, Gabby and Olivia whispered about it. As though Stephanie's panic attacks wouldn't happen if they didn't mention them. Gesturing toward the nearest table, she said, "Have a seat. My coworker, Helen, should be here any minute. I've got my stuff in the back, so we can head out then."

"No worries. We've got severe clear all the way to Seattle."

"You lost me." Shaking her head, she asked, "Severe clear?"

"Sorry. Pilot slang for it's a gorgeous day."

"That," she said with a smile, "I understand."

He chose a sunny corner table, and after delivering his order, she made a coffee for herself—only with a huge dollop of cream and plenty of sugar.

Eyeing her mug, he said, "I should've known you were a lightweight."

She stuck out her tongue, and then sat in the comfy seat across from him. "I can't believe you're here."

"It does feel strange being together outside of Miami. I mean, not *together,* but—" Reddening, he turned his attention toward his cinnamon roll.

"I get it," she said, ducking behind her mug for a sip of coffee. She also got his message—that when it came to a repeat performance of their kiss, it wasn't going to happen.

The bell over the door jingled.

Helen bustled in, both hands filled with shopping bags. She was a stout middle-aged woman with short-cropped black hair and a perpetual smile. "Sorry I'm late getting back. You wouldn't believe the sale at Merrimack's."

"Good, huh?" Stephanie grinned at her pack rat friend.

"Halloween was on clearance, and I got a whole set of ghost china and pumpkin napkin rings to match for practically nothing." With the bags hefted onto the counter, she turned to their guest. "Brady, I presume?"

Rising, he nodded, extending his hand for her shake. "Yes, ma'am. And you must be the infamous Helen?"

Helen flushed. "Has my supposed friend been telling stories on me?"

"Not at all. Just explaining that you're her relief."

"In that case—" she gripped his fingers as if they were candy bars marked down seventy-five percent "—nice to meet you."

Looking from Stephanie to Helen with a mischievous grin, he said, "Why do I get the feeling I'm missing good gossip?"

"With this one?" Hooking her thumb toward Stephanie, Helen snorted. "Boring as they come. Me, on the other hand, I could tell you stories that—"

"Okay," Stephanie said, already on her way to the back room to grab her purse and small satchel, "I'm thinking that's our cue to leave."

"Now?" Feigning disappointment, Brady teased Helen, "This was just getting good."

"She always has been a party pooper," Helen said in regard to her boss.

Ignoring her, Stephanie asked Brady, "Ready?"

He nodded. "Helen, it's been a pleasure."

"Likewise," she noted, ambushing him with a hug. "Mmm. You are a tall drink of water. Been a while since I've had my hands on anything as delicious as you."

"Helen!" Mortified, Stephanie hustled Brady toward the door. "I'll have my cell on if you need anything. And if it gets slow, just close up. Now that it's getting dark so early, I don't like you driving at night."

"Yes, Mom," Helen said with a snappy salute. On their way out the door, Helen added, "Don't do anything I wouldn't!"

"I'm guessing that pretty much leaves the door wide-open?" Brady asked with a wry smile.

"I refuse to discuss it in polite company." Hand on

the small of her back, he led her to the airport courtesy vehicle, an old white station wagon parked at the curb. It had more dents than paint.

"I'm thinking that may be my cue to dump you and take Helen?"

She elbowed him.

Grinning, he took her bags, setting them in the backseat. Opening the passenger side door, he gestured for her to climb in, but when she misjudged the space between the curb and car, she tripped.

"Whoa. I've gotcha." His hands around her waist felt strong and secure. The antithesis of her suddenly haywire pulse. "You okay?"

She nodded. "Lisa talked me into taking my anti-anxiety meds. Guess I'm a little woozy."

"Then I guess it's a good thing I'm the one flying." After getting her safely into the car, he climbed behind the wheel. Stephanie laughed when he turned the ignition and the engine sounded as if it belonged on a tugboat rather than a car.

"You making fun of my ride?"

Enough black smoke belched out of the exhaust to block the rear-window view.

"Maybe."

"Once you see our next ride," he said, pulling away from the curb, "you'll eat your words."

AFTER EASING THE COURTESY vehicle back into its appointed spot at the airfield, Brady turned to Stephanie. Her breathing had deepened and judging by the frequency of her blinks, she was having a tough time staying awake.

"Hey…" He nudged her fully conscious. "Am I that boring that I've already put you to sleep?"

She answered with a politely covered yawn. "Maybe I shouldn't have taken my medicine so soon?"

"You're fine." Out of the car, he walked around to open her door and help her to an upright position before grabbing her bags. "Sleepy beats the hell out of zip ties."

"Heh, heh, heh."

"Sorry. Couldn't resist."

"Try."

Holding open the FBO's door, Brady ushered Steph into the business office where the fueler stood behind a tall counter.

"Afternoon." He tipped his red Razorbacks cap. Though his face had been leathered by age and sun, his welcoming smile didn't look a day over eighteen. "Great day for flyin'."

"That it is," Brady said, setting the car's keys on the counter. "Thanks for the ride."

"Our pleasure." After hanging the keys on the end of a row of wall-mounted hooks, he asked, "Want me to top you off?"

"Please." Brady handed over his Visa.

"Help yourself to the amenities." The man gestured toward an island of modern equipment—computer, phone, fax, copier—in what was otherwise an outdated shed.

"Hang tight over here for a few minutes," Brady said, guiding Steph to a seating area featuring a commercial coffeemaker spitting out heavenly smelling brew. Dark paneled walls provided the perfect background for sagging black sofas and a magazine rack filled with an array of aviation magazines guaranteed to send his companion into a nice, deep slumber. "I'm going to check weather and file a flight plan."

"Okeydoke." Her smile was *off*. Like she wasn't only sleepy, but a smidge pharmacologically toasted.

He found a *Good Housekeeping* and put it in her hands. "Need anything? Something to drink?"

"No, thanks."

He poured black coffee into a china mug, dropped a quarter into the Honor Jar, and then sat at the computer desk to fill out an online flight plan and check the weather.

Finished, he asked Steph, "You going to be all right if I head outside to help with the tie-downs?"

Eyes closed with her chin drooping, she nodded.

If this had been a date, he'd take her napping to be a bad sign, but knowing her history and the struggle she faced with flying, he knew she needed the calming medication.

The sun lied. Even though it was a bright day, cold had settled into the bowl-shaped valley Stephanie called her home. Ramming icy fingers into his coat pockets, he spent a few minutes chatting with the fueler, finalized his gas purchase, and then grabbed his fuel strainer before starting his preflight check. Looking over his inherited Beechcraft Baron 58 never got old. High-gloss white with royal-blue, gold and red accents, she was a sight to behold. Brady missed his uncle Fred but every time he flew, he hoped the old guy was upstairs loving the ride every bit as much as him.

Checking the engine and the nose, Brady wished Steph were with him. It might be useful to her to understand that with proper precautions, flying was as safe—hell, in many ways safer—than climbing in her family car.

Finished, he headed back inside for his passenger.

"Ready?" he asked, giving her shoulder a gentle nudge.

"Mmm…" Her yawn and sleepy stretch was topped off by a drowsy smile. "How long was I out?"

"Only long enough to miss out on all of the work."

"Cool."

"Lucky thing I'm not charging you for this trip or that attitude would have you paying double."

"Sorry. Maybe on the return trip, I'll have more energy."

"Don't sweat it. Although…" He pulled a TransGlobal ball cap he'd picked up at his last training review from his coat pocket. "I was planning on giving you this as a party favor, but now—"

"Ooh!" Suddenly awake, she snatched it from him. "Michael always tried winning me one of those but he was much better at piloting than raffling. Thanks." Loosening the Velcro at the back of the cap, she fit it to her head, and pulled her ponytail out of the back. "I'm good to go."

She sure was. With the exception of his beautiful little girl, his plane had never had a better-looking fare.

"Is that normal?" Stephanie asked about three minutes into their flight. She'd made it through crawling into the cockpit alongside him, survived the terror of leaving the ground, having headphones clamp her head like a vise, and seriously having to pee, only to now grip the arms of her seat tight enough that she was pretty sure she'd leave finger imprints in the fancy leather seats.

"Perfectly." Through the headset, his voice sounded different—infinitely more in control. A good thing. She was in major need of a calming influence! "On a crisp fall day like this, the lower layer of air is bumpier. We're going through the mixing layer. After that, I promise the ride will smooth out."

"If you say so...."

Trying to focus on anything other than the fact that she was hurtling through the sky, by the minute getting farther from her babies, she focused on the plane's swanky decor. Cherry trim and built-in side tables along with navy carpet provided a sumptuous foundation for all of the fawn-colored leather upholstery.

"This is supersweet," she noted, angling on her seat as much as her seat belt allowed. "So remind me again how you came to have it? I mean, not to get personal, but—"

He was forced to cut her off by talking with someone on the radio. Another man, who spouted lots of Alpha/Bravo/Charlie-type lingo that sounded about as foreign to her as one of her more complex phyllo-dough recipes might've been to him. He finished, and his sideways grin stole her breath. "Before we were so rudely interrupted you were saying?"

Shaking her head to clear it of a humming awareness that had nothing to do with the engine's drone, she regrouped. "I was just saying that knowing how little Michael made, unless you've taken up running cargo a little more pricey than passengers, this is out of your league."

"My uncle left it to me. Remember? I thought I told you?"

"You probably did," she said with a flustered smile. "If so, tell me again, because it obviously didn't sink in."

He fiddled with some switches and knobs and then checked a couple of gauges. "My uncle was our family's black sheep. Much to Grandma Rose's dismay, he never even married—just cohabitated, as she called it—with an Anchorage burlesque dancer named Frieda."

"As in Anchorage, Alaska?"

"That'd be the one," he said, checking the radar screen. "So anyway, he dropped out of high school and headed up there when he was seventeen. Filed for a mining claim and hit it big. The rest is history. He died just last year, and believe me, no one was more surprised than me when I got a certified letter informing me that I was now the proud owner of my very own slice of Heaven. When I picked her up, I even got to meet Frieda."

"What was she like?"

"Bawdy. Mountains of red hair and big boobs. And the most wicked-fun personality I'd run across in years. We still keep in touch."

"Cool."

"That your official word of the day?"

"Maybe." She yawned. "Michael would've loved this. He always talked about one day having his own plane. He looked so good in his TransGlobal uniform. Lots of ladies tried catching him, but he always came home to me." Eyelids fluttering with invisible weight, she added, "I could never come close to loving another man as much as him."

Chapter Seven

How much did it suck that here Brady sat at a blaring kiddie concert with some blond-haired, blue-eyed Romeo crooning to his daughter and four of her closest friends, and all he could think about was how irked he still was by Stephanie's earlier comment?

While she danced along with the girls, he glowered, glad for the stadium's dark. Yes, to have even let the innocent statement register on his radar was idiotic. He and Steph were friends. He'd only brought her out here as a favor to his old buddy who wouldn't have wanted his wife forever crippled by a fear of flying.

His conscience snorted. Yeah, right. How much of his invitation had had to do with chivalry and how much with a certain kiss?

Arms tightly folded, he feigned interest in the teen his daughter and her friends squealed over.

"What's wrong?" Steph shouted above an excruciating lead guitar solo.

"Headache," he only half lied.

"Want aspirin?" She'd already reached for her purse.

He shook his head. "Let's get out of here for a minute. Maybe get a hot dog."

She nodded.

To his daughter, he explained the plan.

To which she shouted, "Geesh, Dad, if you want to make out, couldn't you wait until after the show?"

Vowing to deal with Lola's mouth later, he grabbed Steph's hand and led her up narrow stairs heading out of the arena.

"Better?" she asked once distance had somewhat subdued the noise.

He nodded. "I can't believe how much these tickets set me back. It's like I paid to be tortured."

"Lola and her friends are clearly enthralled. Trust me," she assured, "your money was well spent. She'll always remember this night."

Smelling food, he asked, "Hungry? We were in such a rush to pick up Lola and crew from the airport that we didn't get dinner."

"True. I've been wondering if you'd ever get around to feeding me."

They bantered over mustard-slathered hot dogs, Cokes and popcorn. And when that was done, they went back to the concession booth for soft-serve ice cream cones. At arena prices, the meal no doubt cost more than a night out at some swanky steak place, but damned if he hadn't enjoyed himself more. His earlier funk had been replaced by an inexplicable sense of contentedness. As though at least for the next thirty minutes, or so, all was good in his life.

"Not to sound patronizing," he said upon finishing his cone, "but you did great today. Your nerves hardly showed at all."

Dredging the pink tip of her tongue around the base of her treat, she took a long time to answer. "This might sound *out there,* but the whole time we were in the air, I felt like Michael was with me. Assuring me everything would be all right."

Like a raging flash flood, Brady's jealousy over his old pal roared back. Irrational. Downright stupid. But there all the same.

"We had such a great marriage. Michael was crazy about one day becoming a father. I never even got to tell him that we were expecting." Her blue eyes filled with tears. "Sorry. You've shown me the kind of good time I only used to share with him, which is great, but for some reason it's bringing back memories I'd thought were safely locked away."

"We're, ah, cool." He'd striven for a carefree tone. The kind of casual, hip attitude a guy hanging out with his best friend's girl would naturally adopt.

"Thought *cool* was my word," she teased with the cutest little crease between her eyes.

"My bad." Hands flattened into a makeshift serving platter, he *passed* it back to her. "It's all yours."

"Thank you."

"You're welcome."

Extending her small hand toward him, she asked, "Ready to head back in?"

No. But hand in hand they entered the arena. Lucky for him, he still had an hour in the dark left to brood about the forbidden thrill of sliding his fingers between hers.

"SHE'S REALLY PRETTY." Lola padded into his office a little after 2:00 a.m. Her pink lamb pj's weren't anywhere near as cute as her crazy hair.

"What're you doing up?" Swiveling his desk chair to better see her, he abandoned his mindless game of spider solitaire.

"Couldn't sleep. Jenny snores—loud."

He chuckled. "Sorry."

She plopped cross-legged onto the thickly carpeted floor. "It's okay."

Right after the concert, they'd dropped Steph off at her hotel, and then ran the rest of the girls back to his place. He would've lectured Lola on the merits of a good night's sleep, but when his eyes wouldn't shut, either, he could hardly blame the kid. "Want some hot chocolate?"

She nodded.

In the kitchen, they worked as a team, assembling milk, sugar and cocoa the way they had since she'd first learned to stand and her favorite kitchen toy had been a big, plastic spoon. Somewhere in her cluttered room at Clarissa's, she still had it—bite marks and all.

"Did you guys go make out when you left the show?"

"No," he said, more than a little miffed that she even knew what the phrase meant. "Not that it's any of your business, but we got hot dogs and talked about boring stuff like what we think our girls will be when they grow up."

"What'd you tell her I want to be?"

"What else?" He fished in the fridge for the spray bottle of whipped cream. "A drama queen."

"That's so not true." She pretended to be offended, but her barely hidden smile told him that a part of her was proud that he'd noticed her dramatic tendencies. Little did she know he also worried about them! "You know I want to be an Olympic gymnast."

"Yes," he acknowledged with a ruffle to her hair, "I do know, but it's always more fun to tease."

She stuck out her tongue. "I think Mom's gonna be super jealous."

"'Bout what?" He measured milk before dumping it into a saucepan.

"Duh. Stephanie." Hands on her hips, she gave him the you're-such-a-dork look she usually reserved for when he asked questions about one of her gymnastic routines. "That's the only reason you brought her all the way out here, right? So Mom could see some other girl likes you and then she'd be so jealous she'll want you back?"

"SHE DIDN'T," STEPHANIE SAID the next morning over a bayside breakfast of cream cheese–slathered bagels and steaming, legendary Seattle coffee. Aside from Brady's confession that his daughter considered her the ultimate jealousy bait, the morning was breathtaking. She wasn't sure which body of water they currently strolled around, but the combination of salty air, ringing mast lines and the occasional slap of a wave against the boardwalk and marina docks made for a heady overall experience. Toss in Brady's pleasant company and it had been an all-around great morning.

"Oh, yes, she did. Just thought I'd warn you as to why she was giving you all of those squinty-eyed glares."

"Truthfully," she said with a laugh, "I thought she had something in her eye."

"I wish," he grumbled, before taking another bite of bagel. He had a smidge of cream cheese in the corner of his mouth and instinctively, as she might've with Michael, she reached up to wipe it away. In the process, she caught a hint of his breath. Coffee and cream cheese and that little something extra she already recognized as him. Unfortunately, since Brady wasn't her husband, instead of allowing her to preen him, he flinched.

"Sorry," she said, immediately retreating to her own personal space.

"It's okay. I didn't mean to… You know."

She nodded, making a mental note to keep her hands to herself. Being with Brady should be comfortable, but in the same way she would be with any friend. Bumbling through the awkward next few seconds, she said, "Anyway, I'm trying not to leap to conclusions about Lola, but *is* that why you brought me here? In the hopes of making Clarissa jealous? If so, because we're just friends, that's all right—I mean, it's not, but—"

Hand on her forearm, he stopped her cold. "I invited you to my hometown to help get you over your fear of flying, and because I've really missed having a friend from the old days. You know, back before everything in my life went to hell."

"Not everything," she said, sipping her brew and trying to ignore a delicious tingle where his fingers brushed her skin. Was that how it was? He was allowed to touch her, but not the other way around? Or was she overanalyzing his every move because she hadn't been around a man in nearly two years? "Overall," she licked suddenly dry lips, "don't you think you and Lola are growing stronger by the day?"

"I thought so," he admitted, "but hearing her say that about you makes me wonder if all this time I've been fooling myself. What if all of my warm-fuzzies about our new and improved relationship are one-sided?"

"I'm not going to say it isn't possible." Walking again, she tried not focusing so much on her awareness of Brady, but the heady rush of exploring somewhere new. "For what it matters," she said as they passed a guy hosing down his boat, "as a fellow parent, though my girls aren't anywhere near the stage Lola is, I think the fact that you were willing to up and move back to Seattle was a bold step in the right direction. As for her whole make-mom-jealous scheme, relax. It'll blow over." *Just like my urge to comfort you with a big hug.*

Brady's knitted eyebrows told a different story.

"THANK YOU."

"Sure." After returning Stephanie safe and sound and still somewhat sedated to Valley View, Brady climbed out of the airport courtesy vehicle to gather her things and walk her to her front door.

The return flight had been uneventful, leading him to wonder why she'd ever panicked to such a degree.

"Want to come in for a minute? You've got to be beat."

"True," he said. A nap would be great, but it was already getting dark and he still had a long night ahead of him in flying home. "But I should be getting back."

"Michael always tried resting between flights." Though she wore a heavy woolen sweater, she crossed her arms, rubbing herself to ward off the cold.

"A good policy." But Brady had heard enough about his old friend to last him a good, long while. The last thing he wanted to do was chill in the guy's home. Especially since he'd spent a long afternoon musing about how much it sucked being stuck at nine thousand feet for over fifteen hundred nautical miles alongside a sleeping beauty no doubt dreaming of a man other than him. "But I've got things to do back home."

Lightning cracked the western sky.

"That came in faster than I'd expected." Cramming

his hands in his jeans pockets, he was itching to get a hold of a weather report.

A light sprinkle started to fall, making the already nippy autumn air downright frigid.

Jogging to the front door, Steph shouted over her shoulder, "Mother Nature's trying to tell you something…"

"You're probably right," he said as the cold rain fell harder.

Her home was as welcoming as her shop. Small, but cozy with sunny-yellow walls, honey-toned hardwood floors and the kind of feminine, frilly touches he wouldn't have thought Michael would've gone for. An overstuffed floral sofa and love seat nicely blended with a maple china cabinet crammed full of china collectibles. A redbrick fireplace was flanked by built-in bookshelves. An assortment of paperbacks, hardcover novels and even magazines were crammed haphazardly amongst framed photos—mostly featuring Michael or the babies. On the mantel sat a wooden flag case Brady presumed Stephanie had been given at Michael's memorial service. His formal Air National Guard portrait sat alongside it.

In front of a large window sat a playpen, surrounded by stuffed animals and the kind of primary-colored blocks and chubby toys Lola played with when she'd been a baby.

"This is nice," he said.

Outside, the rain fell harder.

Inside, his heart pounded when Steph removed the black velour jacket she'd been wearing to reveal a surprisingly low-cut tank that showed off toned arms and even a peek of belly.

"Thanks." Tugging at her shirt, she tossed the jacket

over the back of a white armchair. "There were a lot of things Michael and I still wanted to do—mostly land-scaping, but..." Darting into the kitchen, she returned moments later with a dish towel, daubing at her face and throat. "I got wetter than I'd thought."

When she offered it to him, he shook his head. "No, thanks."

"Want something to drink? Eat?"

"It's nice of you to offer, but I'm good." As soon as the rain cleared, he was out of here. Standing next to Steph, in Michael's home, he had never been more keenly aware of the fact that the two of them together would be a disaster. Sure, it was peaceful around here now, but once her girls were home, this place would be a madhouse. He'd done the husband thing and failed miserably. Same CD, different track when it came to his parenting skills. He was trying to make things better, but Steph and her babies deserved more.

"It's so quiet with Michaela and Melanie not here." She sat hard on the sofa. "Once this storm clears, maybe I should head down to Little Rock to get them."

"What was the original plan?" he asked, perching on a sofa arm.

"Olivia was bringing them to school in the morning."

"Sounds like a good friend."

"The best." Hand to her throat, Steph glanced away.

What was she thinking? Was she as uptight about him being here as he was?

Pulling out his iPhone, he asked, "You don't mind if I check radar, do you?"

"Please. Do whatever you need." Eyeing her lone suitcase lying on the entry hall floor, she said, "In fact, while you do that, I'll unpack. Once the girls are here, I'll never find time."

With her gone, he told himself the radar was riveting, but in truth, he couldn't help but notice how the place smelled like her. A little sweet. Flowery. Infinitely attractive.

Steph must've turned on her bedroom TV, as the sound of a weather forecast drifted down the dark hall.

The longer Brady sat on his own, watching a line of severe storms blossom into a mess he had no desire to fly into, the more he wondered what the hell he was going to do. Here he was, essentially stuck smack-dab in the middle of Bumpkinville, USA, with a gorgeous old friend. Any sane guy would no doubt find that a good thing. But all it took was one look at the picture on the mantel to remind Brady that no matter how tempting Steph became, this was a *look, don't touch* situation.

"I just saw radar," she said, strolling up from behind him. "Not that I'm an expert, but looks like you're going to be here awhile."

"Yeah." He'd reached the same conclusion. The storm system had been predicted to form far south of the region and not until early tomorrow.

"You're welcome to my guest room." She walked by him, sitting cross-legged on the couch. During the short time she'd been gone, her bra had been disposed of. She still wore the thin, white tank top and when she leaned far to her left to switch on a lamp, her breasts threatened to make an appearance.

Mouth dry, he pressed his lips tight. What the hell had he gotten himself into? "I, ah, don't want to put you to any trouble. If it comes down to it, I can always crash on the plane."

Her face paled.

Catching the gist of what he'd said, he backpedaled. "The dinette folds down into a decent bunk."

She nodded, but it didn't take a rocket scientist to tell his one innocent statement had reminded her of her husband and the way he'd met his demise.

The harder the rain fell, the more difficult it became to find conversation.

Thankfully—at least for him—a steady dripping noise had started in the kitchen, giving them both the opportunity to inspect.

Groaning, Steph covered her eyes with the heels of her hands. "I've known I needed a new roof for a while now, but was hoping to hold off until next summer."

"Maybe it'll stop." As if his hopeful words had dared it to worsen, now, instead of there being a drip, water fell in more of a dribbled stream. "Did Michael have any tools?"

"Sure? Why?" She knelt before a bottom cabinet, removing a bowl to try catching some of the mess.

"It won't last until summer, but how about I put on a patch that will at least stop the leak until morning when you can get someone out here to look at it."

"No," she said with a firm shake of her head. Her one word was punctuated by a fresh roll of thunder. "Absolutely not. If you don't get struck by lightning, you'll catch your death of cold."

"Tools in the garage?" he asked, already headed toward a door tucked into a corner of the kitchen that would no doubt lead that way. "A tarp, staple gun and ladder should have you fixed up in no time."

"Yes, we've got all of that, but—Brady, *please* don't go outside in this." Her voice had taken on an extreme edge. As if a part of her honestly believed he wasn't coming back. The mission was admittedly unpleasant, but the roof's pitch was shallow and he'd always been steady on his feet.

Hand gripping the side of the open garage door, he said, "I'm touched by your concern, but I promise, I'll be fine."

When he turned to glance at Stephanie, he groaned at the sight of her tears.

Chapter Eight

Stephanie fought to keep hold of her composure as she listened to the sound of Brady clomping around on the roof in the middle of a thunderstorm. More than anyone, she knew just how easily promises could be broken. How good intentions had nothing to do with fate deciding it was your turn to *go*.

She'd made coffee, but her hands trembled to such a degree that she gave up on trying to hold the mug.

Pacing, wringing her hands at her waist, praying and praying for the lightning and thunder and rain to stop even though the storm only worsened, Stephanie was on the verge of calling 9-1-1 when the door to the garage opened and then shut.

Relief shimmered through her.

Running to him, not caring that he was dripping head to toe, she hugged him and hugged him and cried hard enough to drown out the storm, if only for a moment. "I—I was so afraid y-you weren't coming back."

With his wet hands, he cupped her face. "Whoa. Where's this coming from? I couldn't have been out there more than fifteen minutes."

"I—I know," she said through hiccups and sniffles, "but Michael promised he'd be back, and—"

"Are you having another panic attack?"

"No." She vehemently shook her head. "I'm over those. Remember how great I did both ways to Seattle?"

"Yeah...but this—Steph, you're not being rational. I suppose something could've happened to me, but if you think about it realistically, the odds were pretty slim."

Even so, she couldn't release her hold on his waist.

"Steph—" one-by-one he pried her fingers away "—you have to let go. I need to dry off, and make sure the tarp stopped the leak."

Fighting the wave of exhaustion that followed extreme fear, she reluctantly let him go.

"I'm not Michael," he said, wiping down his face with a dish towel he'd taken from the counter. "You get that, don't you?"

"Of course. What? Do you think I'm certifiable?"

He paused. "No." When she scowled, he added, "I'm just worried about you. Maybe you need to find someone to talk with. Like a professional."

Turning away, she folded her arms tightly across her chest. "I've been to my family doctor, and she says this sort of thing is perfectly normal."

Heart aching for her, he ran the towel over his hair before wadding it into a ball he pitched into the sink.

"I'm *normal*, Brady. There's *nothing* wrong with me. In fact, what kind of friend would I be if I hadn't been worried about you?"

"You're right." He backed away.

"Come on," she said, needing out of the cramped kitchen and away from his concerned stare, "I'll show you your room and find you dry clothes."

"How about a hot shower?" He knelt to unlace soggy brown leather boots. The socks he peeled off formed small lakes on the linoleum floor.

"Sure." Leading him to the hall bathroom, she handed

him a clean, white terry cloth robe. "Give me all of your wet things, and I'll wash them."

He grunted thanks before closing himself into the hall bathroom.

A minute later, he opened the door a crack. "You out there?"

She took his clothes and retreated to the laundry room, wondering how to best get through the night. Turned out, she needn't have worried, because by the time she finished rounding up enough dark clothes to start his load, he'd already crashed on the guest-room bed.

When her alarm went off at five-thirty, she bolted out of bed, intent on finding him, but the bed was neatly made and Brady was gone. The only proof of him ever having been in her home was a simple note, thanking her for letting him stay.

"YOU'RE THE SMARTEST *ever,*" Brady overheard Lola gushing into her cell phone. He'd just taken a load of towels from the drier and was now in his room, folding.

Though her bedroom door was closed, she talked loud enough that no doubt the neighbors caught her every word, as well.

It'd been a week since he'd left Steph's house in the middle of the night. He'd felt bad about sneaking off, but he'd been rethinking his decision to fly Steph to Seattle. She clearly wasn't ready to move on. He wanted—intended—to help her. But how?

Still in her room, Lola laughed so hard, she snorted. "Everything you said turned out to be right. Dad's like dating this lady, and my mom's like freaking out."

Brady cringed.

Please, God, tell him he hadn't heard what he thought he just had....

"No, for real, Mom was all like asking me what this lady looked like and everything, and even better, Dad was all like buying me anything I wanted. It's great, and I—"

Abandoning the towels, Brady opened the door to his daughter's room. "Give me the phone. Now."

"No way." She covered the mouthpiece. "Dad!"

"Now." He held his hand out, palm up, directly in front of her face.

"Becky, I've gotta go." Flipping her phone shut, she placed it in his hand. "There. Happy?"

"Not even close." Pocketing the phone, he pointed toward the living room. "Step into my office. We're going to talk."

"I was just joking."

If his blood boiled any harder, he'd stroke out.

When a rapid count to ten did nothing to calm him, he changed gears. "On second thought, pack up your stuff. Let's have this conversation with your mother."

"But it's early," she whined. "If I go home now, I'll have to start my science-fair project."

If Brady had his way, she'd be grounded for the next month. Meaning Lola and her volcano study would soon be BFFs.

"NOT ONLY IS SHE FULL OF SASS, Clarissa, but she's manipulative." With their daughter in her room, cleaning out the guinea pig cage she was supposed to have handled before taking off with him on Friday afternoon, Brady stood in the kitchen, his back to the counter, both hands rammed in his pockets. "She needs to be grounded for several weeks."

His ex-wife didn't even slow down with mincing green peppers for a salad. "You can't ground her for more than a few days for general disrespect and dissing your new girlfriend."

"Steph's not my girlfriend. You knew her, too. She needed help and I was there for her."

Clarissa's narrow-eyed glare left no doubt as to where his little girl had picked up her knack for sarcasm. "That why you spent half of Lola's college fund on airplane fuel, flying Stephanie out here?" She grabbed a carrot, now chopping harder.

"You know damned well that part of that inheritance included a fuel stipend."

Still chopping, she rolled her eyes. "Seems like an awful big step on the dating ladder to me."

"You're jealous, aren't you?"

"Not even a smidge. What I am is pissed that you made the poor decision to take what was supposed to have been a special night for Lola and turned it into a make-out session."

"What?"

"Oh—don't even try denying it." Annihilating a cucumber, she added, "Lola told me everything. How you and Steph left the concert and Lola had to go out looking for you once it was over, because—"

"This is B.S. Steph and I left the show for maybe fifteen minutes to grab a hot dog. Lola knew exactly where I was, and I never left the arena. So let's add lying to her list of sins."

"Know what I think?" Clarissa asked, knife still in hand and pointing in his direction.

"Please, enlighten me…"

Ignoring his ticked-off tone, she said, "I think you're

the one lying to cover your sin of using a night out with your daughter for a date."

"Get it through your thick head, what Steph and I shared wasn't a date. And so what if it had been? We both know how it played out between us, Riss. God only knows what you and my brother did in front of Lola."

"Yeah, because you were never here. What was I supposed to do? Raise Lola by myself? But wait, even when you were here, I pretty much did that anyway."

"That's the stupidest thing I've ever heard. When I was home, I was always here for you and Lola."

"Your body might've been here, but that's the extent of it. Emotionally, you'd checked out."

Jaw clenched, Brady struggled for the right comeback. "What else was I supposed to do? You were cheating on me with my frigging brother."

"Face it, Brady, you were a horrible husband. Always leading a double life. You acted as if I was an imposition to your layover extracurricular activities. Once Lola came into the picture, I thought it would get better, but it didn't. Like it or not, your actions drove me to your brother."

"This was such a great surprise." On a bright Sunday morning, Stephanie had parked her minivan in front of the Valley View Municipal Airport, and now hopped out, running a few feet to give Brady a hug. His 7:00 a.m. call, asking if it'd be all right for him to visit, had been as unexpected as it was welcome. It'd been a while since she'd seen him, and truthfully, she was beginning to wonder if he'd ever call again. Her friend Gabby had urged her to make the first move, but in light of the way he'd left in the middle of the night,

Stephanie decided to bow out gracefully. "I thought I'd scared you off."

"Never," he said. "It takes a lot more than crying about late-night roof repairs to make me bolt."

She laughed, which felt remarkably good.

"Speaking of which…" They both headed for the van. "Ever get it properly fixed?"

"Yes, sir."

"Good. I worried about you."

He worried? The notion warmed her.

In the van, he tossed his satchel on the floor behind the passenger seat and then played goofball by formally introducing himself to her girls. "Ladies, I don't have a clue which of you is Michaela and which is Melanie, but regardless, I'm Brady and it's a pleasure finally meeting you."

Always ready to ham it up for a good-looking *boy*, Michaela giggled and cooed. Melanie, however, turned shy, hiding behind her stuffed strawberry squeeze toy.

"I'm glad at least one of them seems not to hate me," he teased.

Smiling, putting the van into Reverse, Stephanie backed out of her space, eager to get started on their fun day. "Sure you don't mind tagging along with us to the zoo?"

"It'll be fun," he assured. "I haven't been in years."

"On a day as pretty as this, it's bound to be crowded. Lucky for us, the girls' stroller doubles as a battering ram."

Glancing over to see him grin, her stomach flip-flopped. Maybe it was just because they shared a confined space, but he seemed bigger than she remembered. Larger than life. Broad shoulders and a strong chest and arms capable of holding her irrational fears at bay.

His dark hair was its usual rumpled mess and though sunglasses hid his brown eyes, her memory of them contributed further to her racing pulse. He might be just a friend, but he was certainly a good-looking one!

"WHAT'RE YOU DOING?" BRADY glanced up to see Stephanie hustling from the restroom. Seated on a picnic bench at a snack concession, he'd been temporarily left in charge and seized the opportunity to introduce the twins to cotton candy. Clearly by the size of their smiles, the sugar had already kicked in.

"They were hungry."

"My friend Olivia's a walking encyclopedia on babies, and she says sugar is a definite no-no at this age. It stays in their mouths and causes tooth decay."

"They barely have any teeth," he was glad to point out.

"Of course they do. You just can't see them."

"Uh-huh…" He fed them each another puff of pink sugar.

Still scowling, she sat alongside him on the bench, seemingly oblivious to the riot her proximity caused inside him. Being here with her and finally getting to meet the twins he'd heard so much about, brought new meaning to the word *confused*. When he'd last seen Stephanie, she'd seemed a bit emotional and nowhere near over Michael's death. Not that he'd ever been one to shy from a friend in need, but with his own issues over Lola, additional drama wasn't on his wish list. What was, however, were many more afternoons wiled away like this. On a deeper level… He couldn't help himself. He had to see her. Make sure she was holding up. Knowing she and her girls were amazing, not even the scent of elephant poop drifting along with a light breeze could bring him down.

At least until another unmistakable smell cropped up...

Nose wrinkled, he looked to the girls. "Is that what I think it is?"

Melanie grinned.

"SORRY ABOUT THIS," STEPHANIE said, pulling her minivan into the garage. The twins had cried the entire way home from the zoo. No amount of kid sing-a-long CDs or teething rings or bottles seemed to help. "Usually they love riding in the car."

"It happens," Brady said, looking a little dazed from the noise. She hoped it hadn't turned him off for making a return trip. Though visiting the zoo with her girls was always a treat, today, the brightness in their eyes when the giraffe leaned extra close to the fence made the outing extra special. "What do you think's the problem?"

"Maybe they're hungry for solid food." Once each of the grown-ups had a baby in arm, Stephanie led the way into the kitchen, placing Michaela in her high chair. The infant quieted, but was still red-faced and huffing.

Melanie did the same. "Ever noticed," Brady said after clicking her safety harness into place, "how babies have this way of looking at you with complete and utter scorn when you finally figure out what it is they've been hollering about? Like they resent you for not getting the memo sooner?"

"As a matter of fact," Steph said laughing, already on her way to the upper cabinet where she stored baby food, "I have noticed. Which is why I'm now hustling to bow to their bidding. Our eardrums have been punished enough."

"Amen." Brady pulled out a chair from the kitchen table, parking it next to Michaela. "I don't think I was ever happier than when Lola was a baby."

"How old was she when Clarissa…"

"Two." Voice taking on a wistful note, he wrapped his pinkie around one of Michaela's springy blond curls. "It was such a fun age. She was into everything. Flipping switches and turning knobs. We were constantly baby proofing."

"Sounds like I'll have my work cut out for me."

"And then some."

A few minutes later, Stephanie joined him, placing divided plates of food on each girl's tray, along with the silver spoons Aunt Olivia had insisted every little girl have. Turning to Brady, she asked, "Want to help feed them?"

Grinning, he snatched up Michaela's spoon. "Thought you'd never ask."

Fifteen minutes later, he had more pureed pork, carrots, yams and blueberries on himself than in the girls' bellies.

"They like you," Stephanie said, holding a spoon up to Melanie's grinning mouth.

Michaela shrieked, bucking and kicking in her high chair.

Her every movement covered him in more goop.

"Is she always this spirited?" he asked.

"Usually not. She especially enjoys the company of boys of all ages. Whenever the girls and I hang out with my friends Dane and Gabby and Olivia and Tag, she gravitates toward the guys." After a few moments of silence, she added, "Makes me wonder if she would've been a daddy's girl."

"Possibly," he said, "but that doesn't mean she loves you any less."

"I know. It just hurts. Thinking of the relationship she and Michael might've had."

Brady wasn't sure how to reply. Or even if more talk was necessary. All three Olmstead ladies had landed a rotten deal by losing the man of their family. The thought of which made his own situation—having been easily replaced—all the more aggravating.

"Okay," Steph said once Melanie joined her sister in slapping more food in her wooden high-chair tray than eating. "Looks like you two are full. Time to clean up."

"Need help?" Brady asked, already popping the tray from Michaela's seat.

"Absolutely."

ONCE BATH TIME HAD BEEN finished, and together they'd read stories to the girls and then tucked them snugly into their cribs, Stephanie gestured for Brady to leave the nursery. She followed, closing the door behind her.

In the living room, while Brady collapsed onto the sofa, she picked up the toys the girls had scattered before their outing.

"Don't you ever relax?" he asked, patting the seat alongside him.

"Sometimes." She sat next to him, but not too close. While feeding the twins, his proximity had been disconcerting. His citrus and leather scent too delicious for words.

"Like when?" he prodded with a breathtaking smile.

"I mean, I get that you probably do lots of stuff like today, but what do you do for you?"

"I used to read or knit, but lately, I'm so exhausted after putting the girls to bed that I usually veg out in front of the TV."

"Sounds fun." His deadpan tone told a different story.

"Oh—" Angling to face him, she asked, "What do you do that's so much more entertaining?"

"Let's see…" He stretched his legs out and rubbed his chest. "After downing a few fast-food burgers, I might play a little PS3 or devour the owner's manual of Boeing's 787 Dreamliner."

Laughing, she said, "That's some serious entertainment."

"Have you learned everything you should about the Rolls-Royce Trent 1000 engine?"

Still grinning, she shook her head.

"All right, then. Case closed." Locking his fingers behind his head, he closed his eyes and yawned. "I forgot to add that in my off-time, I'm a professional power napper."

"Really? That's quite a feat. Mind giving me a few pointers?"

"First," he said, rising from the sofa. "You'll need to stretch out—like this." Grasping her ankles, he playfully manhandled her into a reclining position.

"Whoa!" she shrieked, caught off guard.

"Next, you've gotta get something beneath your head. Like this." From the love seat, he took a throw pillow and stuffed it under her head. "Now, do away with those shoes." He yanked off her white canvas Keds sneakers, tossing them to the carpet. "Hmm," he said, glancing around the room, "you need just one more thing."

"What?" she asked, rolling onto her side.

"A blanket. Got one?"

Grinning over his antics, she said, "Hall closet. Top shelf."

"Too far for convenience," he grumbled, already headed that way. "You'll need a lot of training."

A minute later he was back, tossing a faded old quilt over her, tucking it snug around her feet.

"Mmm…that feels good. Thanks."

"You're welcome. But we're not done yet."

"Seems perfect to me." She closed her eyes and sighed. "What else could I need?"

He planted a kiss to her forehead. "Sweet dreams. Now, you get some much-deserved rest and I'll forage for our dinner."

Contentment didn't begin to describe Stephanie's mood. For the first time in what felt like decades, she was warm and safe and not alone. Too bad all of it was temporary. On the ride to the zoo, he'd made it clear that he was only in town for the day. He'd begged the use of her guest bed and an early-morning shuttle to the airport, but aside from that, his presence in her life was about as certain as the chaotic fall weather.

"Brady?" she called out.

"What's up?" He peeked from the kitchen.

"Why are you here? What do you want from me?"

"That came from left field." Perched on the edge of the couch, absentmindedly rubbing her feet through the blanket, he seemed oblivious to the havoc he caused her seesawing emotions. Which only proved why she needed to know.

"Not really," she said. "Put yourself in my shoes. Here's a great guy from my past, admittedly not looking for a relationship, yet here you are… The poster boy for domestic bliss. All I'm asking is why?"

"I get what you're saying," he said, frowning with a fierce mask of concentration. "Trouble is—I honestly don't know."

Chapter Nine

"This is amazing," Stephanie said, swallowing a mouthful of Brady's ham-and-cheese omelet. In the thirty minutes she was supposed to have been napping, she'd dwelled on his answer—or, lack thereof. In the end, though it may not have been the touchy-feely admission she'd secretly hoped for, she admired his honesty. She'd needed it to bring reality back to her life. The two of them shared no great passion and never would. "I've always loved having breakfast for dinner."

"Me, too." Brady speared a piece of egg with his fork. "When I was a kid, we used to have pancakes on Thursday nights. We'd take turns going around the table, talking about anything that interested us, or assigned topics like who most inspired us."

"How fun." Helping herself to seconds on country potatoes, she asked, "Who was your biggest inspiration?"

"Hands down, Amelia Earhart. I know she was a chick and all, but she fascinated me. Still does. I liked how she combined flying with adventure."

"Not bad for a 'chick,'" Stephanie said with a chuckle. "Do you see your parents often?"

He shrugged. "Depends."

"On what?"

His expression clouded.

"Another touchy subject?"

Sighing, he said, "More like complicated. Too much for this close to bedtime. Let's just say I see Mom and Dad about as much as I see Lola."

"O-kay." Stephanie forced a deep breath. "Speaking of your little angel, did you ever have a *talk?*"

He took a while to answer. "This kills me to admit, but when it comes to my kid...I'm clueless. Long story short, she admitted everything—calling you, being extra nice to me so I'd agree to date you. Wanting to make Clarissa jealous... The list goes on and on." He covered his face with his hands. "I confronted her with Clarissa and there was a big, ugly scene. I wanted Lola grounded from her phone and TV and friends for the rest of her life. Clarissa balked—protesting that I obviously didn't know the first thing about parenting."

"Oh, Brady..." Her heart went out to him. The Clarissa she remembered had been reasonable. What changed? "I'm so sorry. Not that it helps, but the rest of Lola's life seems a bit extreme. Clarissa probably has more experience with this sort of thing. Is there anything I can do?"

"Thanks for the offer, but I'm guessing the only thing that'll help is time. In retreating like I did from both Clarissa and Lola's daily lives, I screwed up—big-time. Sure, I might be back now, but they seem to resent it."

"What about Lola's stepfather? What part does he play in all of this?"

Expression hard, Brady said, "None."

STEPHANIE WAS USED TO getting up early, but four was a stretch even for her. From behind the wheel of her minivan, she covered a yawn.

The girls were snug and sleeping in their car seats.

Brady next to her, the space felt unbearably tight. As though there wasn't enough air. By this time, she felt as if she'd known him forever, and yet it had never been clearer that she didn't really know him at all. There was so much she still wanted—needed—to know before saying goodbye. Goofy things like whether he preferred pulp in his orange juice, or what brand of soap he used that made him smell so irresistible. Then there were the important things. Like whether or not he'd ever be whole again.

In losing his wife and daughter, she didn't blame him for being bitter, especially since he hadn't really lost them at all.

"Need help turning the key?"

She glanced his way then smiled shyly. Oh—she needed help, all right. "Thanks. But I'm good."

After making the ten-minute drive in companionable silence, Stephanie pulled in front of the glorified shed serving as the town's airport. Lights glowed inside, so she assumed Brady wasn't the only one with an early-morning departure.

"I feel funny just leaving you here." She put the car in Park.

"Why?" Brady asked, unsure what to do with his hands. He hadn't felt this awkward since taking Kim Shelton to senior prom.

"Never mind. It's stupid."

"Try me," he said, removing his seat belt so that he could angle to face her. As usual, her hair was a crazy nest of corkscrews. In the glow from the parking lot lights, her face looked angelic. Something about her was infinitely approachable. As if he could tell her anything.

"Well..." She licked her lips, adding a gloss to them that inexplicably tightened his groin. "I was just worried you might be lonely. You know, being in the air by yourself. But then it occurred to me that you spend your life doing that, so it must not bother you, and I'm being silly to even wonder about it."

"Maybe," he said, "but I've gotta tell you that's the nicest thing anyone's wondered about me in an awfully long time."

Running her fingertips along the steering wheel's grooves, she said, "I suppose since I'm already up, I should head to the pastry shop."

"So that's my cue to beat it, huh?"

She flushed. "I didn't mean—"

"You're not very good with teasing, are you?" he asked, fighting the urge to cup her cheek.

"No. That's more my sister's thing. You might like her better."

"Uh-uh," he said with a vehement shake of his head. "I'm liking you just fine."

Exhaling, she seemed more than a little relieved he hadn't taken her up on her suggestion. "Would it be all right if I gave you a hug?"

Her ridiculous question made him bust out in a laugh.

"I didn't mean that to be funny," she said. "In fact, I—"

He silenced her by not only pulling her into a hug, but kissing the top of her sweet-smelling head. "And I didn't mean to laugh. I've been wondering if I should give you a hug, so your question struck me as funny."

"Oh." Drawing back, he found her also sporting a smile.

"All right..." He opened his door. "I better go."

"Thanks for visiting. I had fun."

"Me, too." With everything in him, he wanted to kiss her—properly kiss her, but he didn't. Couldn't. For the umpteenth time, he reminded himself the two of them were just friends. "Bye."

Brady waved and then shoved his hands in his jeans pockets, brooding at the sight of her van's fading taillights.

Cold wind bit his exposed skin.

Rustling leaves from across the road mixed with the sound of a far-off barking dog.

The time with Steph and her girls had been torture. Bittersweet. Reminding him of all the family times he'd missed. How had Lola spent her Sunday? Finishing homework? Watching one of her favorite movies or TV shows? Saddest part was that even with him back in Seattle, the two of them were still so distant he didn't know what her favorites were.

Ignoring a shiver, he braced himself against the wind, welcoming its teeth. Maybe physical pain would drown out the emotional.

He'd had so much weighing on him that at times it felt intolerable. But then Stephanie had appeared, giving him the kick in the pants he'd needed to realize he wasn't the only one hurting.

A good thing, right?

But now that he'd gotten to see Steph in her daily life, he didn't feel better, but worse. He now bore the additional worry of her working too many hours, and not seeing enough of her girls. He worried about her little house, and if her roof was in such bad shape, what else was lurking that couldn't be seen? A water heater waiting to gasp its last breath? A sink about to clog?

Clamping his hand to his forehead, he forced a deep

breath. Lord, here he was a bachelor who, aside from
his daughter, shouldn't have had a care in the world. So
why now did he feel as if he'd inherited another man's
family?

"YOU NEVER TOLD ME THAT," Lisa complained while
she and Stephanie jogged their way around Lake Win-
slet. Though the sky was gray and the wind sharp,
Stephanie had needed out of the shop. Or maybe more
specifically, away from her thoughts of Brady.

"I don't have to tell you everything," Stephanie said,
thighs screaming from the first exercise other than man-
ning the vacuum, that she'd had in a while. "It was no
big deal. Brady just got all macho and climbed on top
of my roof in the middle of a storm. I cried a little. End
of story."

"Mmm-hmm..."

"What?" They dodged a honking flock of geese fighting over a discarded hot dog bun. "It wasn't like another
panic attack, or anything. I'm over those."

"If that's truly the case, I'm glad."

"But? Why can't you ever just be happy for me? Even
if what happened two weeks ago had been a true attack,
I survived, didn't I? And obviously Brady thinks I'm
normal or he wouldn't have come back for a second
visit."

"True..." With Stephanie taking a slight lead, they
rounded the playground area marking the halfway point
around the trail. The sky had grown darker, looking as
if at any minute they'd be plagued by a flood.

"All right, out with it. What's got you so snarky?"

"I'm hardly snarky. Just concerned."

"About?" Stephanie snapped. Just once, couldn't her

sister have a normal conversation without being worried about something?

"You sound like you're falling for the guy."

"I'm not. But even if I were, why can't you be happy for me? Brady would make some woman a great catch."

"Except for his kid issues and ex-wife issues, and especially in your case, the fact that he spends a huge portion of his life in a cockpit."

Stephanie might barely be able to breathe, but she did manage to gasp, "I should've asked someone else to go jogging with me. You're a pill."

IT WAS A GOOD THING Stephanie had no romantic feelings for Brady, because when he called two days later, asking to spend a portion of a seventy-two-hour layover with her and the girls, she might've turned him down. As it was, she couldn't have been more pleased.

After picking him up from the airport, she drove to the town square, and with the girls strapped into their stroller, they set off at a casual pace to explore the fall festival being sponsored by local businesses and churches.

I missed you, her racing pulse wanted to say, but in an effort to keep things cool between them, she opted for "Nice night, huh?"

"Beautiful." His easy grin stole her breath away. Gaze locking with hers, he layered meaning upon meaning into his lone word.

She wanted more than anything to take his hand into hers. Instead, she tightened her grip on the stroller handle.

Ludwig's, a German restaurant famous for delicious bratwurst, had sponsored a band and the upbeat

Bavarian tunes set a lively tone for the night. Along with great music were heavenly smells of everything from sausages to funnel cake and caramel-laced apple pie.

"I love that game," Brady said, stopping in front of an apple-bobbing booth. With the earnings going to Valley View Elementary School, he'd at least get soaked for a good cause.

"You just can't stay dry, can you?" she teased when after his third attempt, he still hadn't won.

"I'm doing this for you," he said, eyeing a row of gaudy wooden shoes being given away for prizes. "I want to see you in that hot-pink pair."

"At the rate you're going, fat chance."

Hair dripping, he grinned up at her, "Oh, them's fightin' words."

She should've kept her mouth shut as he won the next round.

After pointing to the bedazzled pink pair featuring yellow and white polka dots, he proudly passed them along to her. "Cinderella, I believe you were missing these?"

She groaned. "You don't really expect me to wear those?"

He nodded. "*Please*...I worked so hard for them."

"You're a hateful, hateful man. You know that, don't you?"

"Stop the chitchat and put on the shoes."

Not wanting to come off as a poor sport, she put on the shoes. "Joke's on you," she teased, doing a silly jig. "These feel great."

"They're looking pretty great, too." His wink struck her as suspiciously flirty.

"Why, Mr. McGuire, you wouldn't be flirting with me, would you?"

Hand to his chest, he feigned shock—and a thick Southern drawl. "Gracious, no, little lady. I'm just workin' my considerable charm."

"Uh-huh." Elbowing him, she dragged Brady off to the concession stand.

"I CAN'T REMEMBER THE LAST time I've had more fun," Brady said while helping Steph carry the girls in from the car. In order to drive, she'd traded her wooden shoes for her sneakers, but his mind's eye recalled all too clearly how cute she'd looked wearing them. She was short, but perfectly proportioned with curves in all the right places.

"Me, too." While unlocking the kitchen door, Melanie fussed and squirmed in Steph's arms.

"Told you we should've fed them more funnel cake."

Giving him the evil eye over her shoulder, Steph said, "Were you volunteering to stay up with them all night when they have gurgling tummies?"

He winced. "Point well-taken."

After Steph flipped on the kitchen's overhead lights, Brady pressed the garage-door button, sending it into a noisy descent.

With Melanie already in her high chair, Brady followed Steph's lead by getting Michaela set up to eat.

"Your booth at the festival was amazing," he said, making small talk while she nuked the girls' food. "Helen scares me, but I liked how all of your cookies were leaf-shaped and colored. You've got skills."

"Thanks." As if she weren't used to praise, she blushed. "Helen's harmless and her humor just takes getting used to. She helped a lot. Plus my three part-time gals."

"Maybe so, but you were the brains."

"Stop." Her pinched look meant business. "What's up with you tonight?"

"What do you mean?"

She took the divided baby plates from the cabinet beside her. "Last time we hung out, it was no big deal. Casual, you know? Like friends should be. But tonight…" Reddening, she fanned her cheeks. "You seem different."

"How?"

After a deep breath, she said, "Like you've forgotten that we're not dating."

"Oh—like you forgot? Have you seen some of the thousand-watt smiles you've cast my way?"

She reddened.

"You do know that was a joke, don't you?"

Hand to her chest, she finally cracked a smile. "I just…well, I never meant for you to get the wrong impression. Like I was hitting on you. Your visits mean the world to me. And I want you to keep coming. But you also need to know that I *get* that you're not available. I'm not looking for some knight to charge up and save me. I'm a big girl and have already saved myself."

"Did I ever say you hadn't?" Taking the plates from her hands and setting them on the counter, he drew her into a hug. "Michael would be so proud of the way you've held things together."

"Th-thank you," she said on the heels of a sniffle.

Tipping back her chin, he asked, "You're not going to start the waterworks again on me, are you?"

Blasting him with a smile that did naughty things below his belt, she shook her head.

Michaela kicked in her high chair.

Melanie followed up with a squeal.

Stephanie gave him one last indecipherable look before taking the plates, setting them in front of the microwave. "Guess that's our cue to start serving."

After feeding the girls, it was time for their bath. Kneeling in front of the tub beside Steph, Brady felt like an old pro. It was amazing how fast infant-care procedure was coming back. And the more he was around Stephanie's twins the more he ached for his own little girl. Trouble was she wasn't little anymore.

The bathroom was girly, like the rest of the house. The white tub and toilet were softened by a pink shower curtain. The girls sat in pink infant tubs, surrounded by plastic bowls and blocks.

"These kids need some real toys," Brady noted, remembering Lola's vast array of tub gear. "I don't see any foamy soap or squirting fish."

"They're only ten months old," Stephanie said, scrubbing Melanie's wispy hair.

"You're never too young to develop a love of squirting things." Making a face, he added, "That came out wrong."

Grinning, she said, "You think?"

They scrubbed in silence for a while. Passing each other the shampoo and taking lots of play-breaks. The swishing of the water and the happy gurgles from the babies filled Brady with bone-deep contentment. Not a good thing considering he had to fly out first thing in the morning.

Voice small, Steph said, "I used to dream of doing this sort of thing with Michael."

"Clarissa was never big on bath time. That was my domain."

"So instead of sharing Lola's care, you two divided and conquered?"

"Guess that's one way of looking at it." Lifting Michaela from the tub, he wrapped her in a fluffy white towel he'd snagged from a pile on the counter. "There were some things we did together. Taking Lola on neighborhood walks. Eating meals."

After pulling a rubber stopper from the tub, Stephanie plucked Melanie from her safety seat and wrapped her in a towel. "Sounds like you led a nice life. How did you find out Clarissa had been cheating?"

Crossing the hall to the twins' nursery, he said, "Might be cliché, but her cell kept getting hang-up calls. Clarissa blew them off, but it irked the hell out of me that some guy was harassing my wife."

"What'd you do?" Stephanie asked, placing Melanie on the pad of an oak changing table to lotion and diaper.

"What else? Called the number. I felt like a fool when I recognized the voice on the other end." Absentmindedly nuzzling Michaela's downy hair, he said, "It was my brother. Calling from a throwaway phone."

"Oh, Brady…" She froze midway through easing Melanie's legs into a pair of soft-looking pink pj's. "When you told me another man was raising your daughter, I had no idea…"

"Yeah, well, it's not something I typically brag about." He swallowed a stupid knot in his throat.

"Still," she said, snapping the legs of Melanie's pajamas, "does it give you any comfort knowing that Lola's at least with family?"

Snorting, he asked, "You're kidding, right?"

"No…"

Swiping his free hand through his hair, he searched for the right place to start. How did one begin to describe how bad it hurt not only having had his younger brother steal his wife, but his daughter, too?

"Look, Brady, I'm sorry, okay? Obviously, I said the wrong thing, and—" she put Melanie in her crib, and then took Michaela from him "—the last thing I wanted to do was cause you more pain."

"I appreciate your apology," he managed, "but would you be particularly grateful if Michael hadn't died, but left you for Lisa? Adding insult to injury by also snagging your kids?"

"I said, I'm sorry. What more do you want?" She lotioned and diapered Michaela and then pulled on her yellow pj's.

What did he want? Nothing.

Because, really, what could she do? He wasn't in the market for a girlfriend to hold him through lonely nights, and he sure as hell didn't need another wife. So why was he even here? Clearly, this slice of domestic bliss was messing with his head. "Now that the girls are down, do you mind if I take a walk?"

"No, but…" She tucked in Michaela. "Please, Brady, accept my apology. I don't like this angry side of you."

"Join the club," he whispered, not wanting to disturb the girls who were already asleep.

Chapter Ten

"Are you okay?" Stephanie asked Brady from the front porch. Baby monitor in hand, she'd wrapped a quilt around herself to ward off the cold.

"Sorry. But you pushed some buttons back there that I'm not equipped to deal with." He stood in the spot she and Michael had dreamed of planting a Chinese maple. The glow from a streetlight showed his profile to be hard. Shut down, as if he'd emotionally checked out.

"Not to butt into your business," she said, "but did it ever occur to you that the reason this thing with your brother and Clarissa is still such a sore point is because you refuse to deal with it?"

He held his lips clamped shut.

"In fact—small-world thing here—but you know my friends Gabby and Dane?"

Nodding, Brady asked, "What about them?"

"Dane's not the father of Gabby's first son—his little brother is."

Eyes narrowed, Brady asked, "You mean to tell me that Dane broke up Gabby's first marriage?"

"Well…" Snuggling deeper into the blanket, it occurred to Stephanie that maybe she'd used the wrong couple for an example. "Gabby wasn't exactly married.

In fact, Dane's younger brother left her just as soon as he found out she was pregnant."

"That's messed up."

"True. Dane kinda, sorta rescued her."

Brady spun around to face her. Gazes locking, she noted that his expression had grown darker than ever. "So then how does that in any way relate to what my brother did to me? Clarissa and I were happily married. Raising our daughter. Vince couldn't stand the fact that I had something he didn't, and he systematically set out to destroy it."

Crossing to him, she stepped gingerly on the spiky grass, wishing she'd slipped on shoes. "You might not want to hear this, but in all of your ranting about how wronged you were, did you ever stop to think about the fact that if Clarissa had been so happy with you, she wouldn't have wanted to stray?"

Brady sharply exhaled. "Have a swell life, Steph. It's been nice knowing you." Taking out his cell, he began to call information for the number of a cab company.

"Wait." Before he could dial, she reached out, snagging him by his shirtsleeve. "I know that was the last thing you wanted to hear, but don't you want to feel normal again, Brady? I mean, I've seen glimpses of the man you're capable of being and you're a keeper. Not the kind of guy a woman would easily toss away. Think about it. Let go of your resentment long enough to really look at your marriage. What went wrong?"

He wrenched himself free and hit the autodial button on his phone. "I need to go."

"Then, go." Softening her tone, she said, "I know it's got to hurt, but—"

"Where do you get off? You don't know anything about my situation. And you're hardly in a position to play marriage counselor when you practically fall apart at the mention of Michael."

"That's low. Like—" she covered her stinging eyes with her hands "—I can't even believe you just said that. You're an ass. You're nothing like the man I met in Miami."

"Damn straight." He covered the mouthpiece of his phone. "Meaning the sooner you get away from me, the better."

BRADY HATED HIMSELF FOR WHAT he'd just done, but sometimes self-preservation was a necessary evil. He'd gone inside for his overnight bag, but then waited on the porch for his cab.

At the airport, he'd roused the sleepy caretaker to top off his tanks and then made quick work of checking the weather and filing a flight plan. Thirty minutes later, he'd been in the air, headed home—not that at the moment, Seattle felt any more welcoming than Valley View.

Having reached cruising altitude, he set the autopilot and squeezed his eyes shut. Fought off a wave of anger so great that it made him sick to his stomach. What had he done to deserve this? To meet an amazing woman like Stephanie and then be so messed up that he couldn't even carry on a decent conversation? Her daughters were angels—as pretty as their mother.

Midway through his second bath time spent with them, warning bells had pealed. Telling him in no uncertain terms that he was in too deep. He'd never intended to tell Steph about Vince. It was not only infuriating, but embarrassing.

"HE LEFT JUST LIKE THAT?" Gabby asked three days later. In honor of Gabby's birthday, Olivia was treating herself, the birthday girl and Stephanie to the works at a Little Rock spa. They currently shared a mud bath.

The babies were all with Olivia and Tag's sitter back at their house while Helen manned the pastry shop.

"Yep," Stephanie said, drawing rapidly dissolving smiley faces in the mud.

"He didn't say goodbye or anything?" Olivia probed. With her long red hair piled on top of her head, she was the only woman Stephanie knew who managed to look elegant while sitting in mud.

"Nope." Honestly, couldn't they just leave it alone? Stephanie loved her friends, but sometimes they acted as though her personal life was as exciting as a pair of Coach shoes marked down for clearance! "Did I tell you that Melanie pulled herself up next to the sofa?"

"I was there when she did it," Olivia said, "and nice try at changing the subject, but it's not going to work. Lindsay Flanders told me at Junior League that your pilot won you the prize her daughter had been eyeing at the Fall Festival. She also said *he* was seriously hot."

Stephanie rolled her eyes. "Brady and I were just friends. Heavy emphasis on the *were*."

"Sure," Gabby said, flicking Stephanie with mud. Sometime during the soaking process, her ponytail holder had snapped, leaving her long black hair plastered to her neck and shoulders. "And I'm leaving Dane to become a nun."

"I'm not surprised. Your husband can be kind of bossy," Steph pointed out.

Gabby frowned.

"All kidding aside," Olivia said, "did you all fight? Is that why he left so abruptly?"

"Yes, we fought. I don't even remember what I said

to tick him off, but you know how I told you his wife left him for another man?"

Her friends nodded.

"Well, turns out, that man was his brother. And he wasn't nearly as noble as Dane was with Gabby."

Olivia whistled. "That had to be tough. But if he volunteered the information, why was he mad at you?"

"Beats me," Stephanie said with a shrug, hoping her friends wouldn't notice the heat rising in her cheeks. The more she thought about it, the more ashamed she felt for pushing him too far. Had she been a true friend, she never would've asked what he'd done to drive Clarissa away. Whether he'd been to blame for their marriage falling apart, or not, she'd been cruel to put the topic on the table.

"Are you going to call him?" Gabby wanted to know.

"I think not." Cupping warm mud in her palm, she let it trickle between her fingers.

"Why?" Olivia asked.

"For starters, because he obviously wants nothing to do with me. Then there's the fact that he lives a thousand miles away. And how about me never having time to spend with my girls, let alone some guy from my past who was better off staying there?"

"All excellent points," Gabby said, "but you left out the most important."

"What might that be?" Steph asked, not really wanting to know.

"Since you inquired," she said with a wink to Olivia, "you failed to mention what everyone in our social circle is buzzing about."

"Our social circle?" Sighing, Steph rose. "That's my cue to get out."

"Not so fast." Gabby grabbed her arm. "All I was going to say is that no less than six of your friends who saw you two at the Fall Festival have called. They want to know who the guy is who brought back your smile."

WITH THE WIND HOWLING outside the nursery, Stephanie rocked her girls to sleep that night and tried to forget Gabby's last comment.

"Ladies," she said, kissing the crown of Michaela's head and then Melanie's, "what do you think I should do?"

Big help they were—both had fallen asleep. Not that she'd expected them to be, but it would be nice when they were old enough to strike up an intelligent conversation.

Rocking and rocking, she tried getting a handle on the confusion clouding her brain.

Gingerly rising, she put each girl in her crib, kissed and tucked, and then flipped on a pink lamb nightlight before turning off the dresser lamp.

In the living room, she turned on the TV, but found nothing good to watch.

She picked up a book she'd been meaning to finish, but the biography of Lady Bird Johnson wasn't exactly riveting.

In the kitchen for a snack, she made microwave popcorn to go along with a diet root beer.

Never had three minutes taken so long. Especially since all she could focus on was the wall-mounted phone.

Should she call him?

If she did, what would she say? An apology for her part of their argument was probably in order, but what then? What did she expect from him? As much as Stephanie hated to admit it, Lisa was right in that she had no business growing attached—even in a friendly way—to another pilot. Then there were his issues with Lola and his ex-wife. Truly, his leaving had been for the best.

The phone stared at her.

Mocked her.

Called her chicken.

Usually, she was immune to name-calling—especially when coming from an inanimate object. But this was different. If she'd learned anything from her in-flight meltdown, it was that it was high time she faced her problems rather than hiding from them. She wasn't supermom or superwoman. If she'd done like her doctor had suggested and taken a light sedative before flying, she never would've gotten herself in such a mess. On the flip side, she wouldn't have met Brady again. A man who, for whatever reason, had gotten under her skin.

"Fine," she said, hands on her hips, staring at the phone. "You wanna play hardball, let's go."

Marching into the living room, she found her purse on the table by the front door. After fishing out her wallet, she found Brady's number on the back of a grocery store receipt right where she'd left it.

In the kitchen, she gripped the phone's handset, punching in her only tangible link to the man.

It rang five times before an answering machine picked up. *Hey—you've reached Brady. You know what to do.*

At the beep, Stephanie hung up.

"IT MIGHT BE FUNNY NOW," Clarissa said, slipping her arm around Lola and giving her a squeeze, "but at the time, I was ready to wring your cute little neck. There were bubbles everywhere."

While on one side of his parents' Seattle family room Brady's ex droned on about their daughter's latest escapade involving laundry detergent and the dishwasher, he tried focusing on his mother, Gloria, who was extolling the wonders of Heath, her new personal trainer.

"He worked me so hard," she said, fanning her face while she talked, "I thought my arms were going to fall off of my body."

"That's nice," he said, trying to eavesdrop on Clarissa.

"It was hardly nice," she scolded. "More like agony. Agony I had to pay for. Your father's livid. Charles says I'm trying to be sixteen again, but honestly, is it wrong for me to want to look my best?"

"Mom?" he asked, envying the way Clarissa and Vince shared the sofa with Lola sandwiched between them. They'd eaten Thanksgiving dinner around three that afternoon, and after the guys had cleaned the kitchen, the whole family was lounging in his parents' family room, watching football. He was so annoyed he hadn't even noted who was playing. "Would you mind getting out of here for a minute?"

"Like where?" she asked, eyebrows raised. "It's a holiday."

"I don't mean leave the house, but get out of *here*. Away from—" He cocked his head in the direction of Clarissa and Vince.

"Come on," his mother said, pulling him by the arm to her upstairs craft room. It used to be a guest bedroom, but now that he and Vince had moved out, there was more than enough space for his folks to spread out their hobbies.

Once she sat in her rolling desk chair, and he was on the love seat, she demanded, "Out with it. You've had a scowl all day."

"Sorry."

Sorting a pile of yarn, she said, "Makes no matter to me. More pie and turkey leftovers."

"Love you, too." Grabbing a pincushion, he busied his hands with pulling pins out and then sticking them back in.

"You know what I mean," she soothed, patting his knee. "Come on, hon. Tell me what's wrong."

Where did he start? Ever since his angry words with Stephanie, he hadn't been right. Sure, he performed his job with the same faultless attention to detail he always had, but in his off-time, he'd felt as if his life was aimless. Like he had no beginning or end to his days. No purpose other than getting through.

"Brady…"

"I'm in trouble, okay?"

Her expression clouded with worry. "Are you sick? Being laid off?"

"No," he said with a firm shake of his head. "Nothing like that." After giving his mom the highlight reel of how Stephanie and her girls had come into his life, he got to the heart of the matter. "So here we were having this idyllic night with her kids, but then it hit me. What was I doing? Playing house with another man's kids? A *dead* man's kids." Pressing the heels of his hands against closed eyes, he said, "Somehow it came out that Vince was responsible for what happened between Clarissa and I, and—"

"Stop right there," she said, putting her newly formed yarn ball on her worktable. "Do you honestly believe it was solely Vince's fault for what happened to your marriage?"

"Hell, yeah," he answered. "You don't?"

She took too long to answer.

"So what did I do besides love my wife and little girl?"

Lips pressed tight, she began a new yarn ball. "I'm not the right person for this conversation, Brady. You know I love you, but what happened between you, Vince and Clarissa is none of my business."

He snorted. "If you're part of the family, you're part of the problem."

"What's that supposed to mean?" Increasing her pace on yarn rolling, she noted, "It wasn't me who worked ungodly hours for years. It wasn't me who asked your brother to watch after your family while you were gone. Vince was doing you a favor, and what happened—while I don't condone it—was the natural outcome of a man and a woman raising a child together. Vince didn't steal your wife, son. You gave her away."

"BRADY?" STANDING AT the open front door in her robe, Stephanie had a tough time believing he was really there. It was seven in the morning, the Sunday after Thanksgiving. The sky was gray, threatening sleet, freezing rain or snow. Weather forecasters said it was a toss-up as to what might fall. "What're you doing here?"

"Sorry," he said, brushing past her when she gestured for him to come in from the cold.

His cab drove off.

"I know I should've called, but I've been flying for days, and saw there was an early flight out for Little Rock, and—"

With Brady inside, out of the cold, Stephanie closed

the door and pulled him into a hug. All anger was gone. In its place a quivery sense of relief. "I tried calling, but—"

"I'm sorry. I haven't even been home."

"It's all right." The longer he held her, the better she felt. He smelled of the damp outdoors. Of sweet wood smoke from a neighbor's fire. The leather of his jacket.

"I feel terrible about how defensive I was with you," he said, his words mingling with his warm exhalations into her hair. "I couldn't wait to see you. Explain."

Nodding against the wall of his chest, she said, "I called to apologize. I shouldn't have needled you. What happened between you and Clarissa is none of my business."

Releasing her, he tucked flyaway curls behind her ears. "By bringing up the subject, I made it your business."

"Doesn't matter," she said, helping him remove his coat. "I just want to go back to us being friends."

"Me, too," he said, catching her gaze and holding it longer than usual. He looked hungry for something. But what? "How are the girls?"

"Snoozing," she said, covering a yawn. "Finally. They were up most of the night tag-teaming me with wet diapers and hungry wails." She sat cross-legged on the sofa, patting the cushion next to her.

"How do you do it?" he asked on his way over. "Clarissa and I used to take turns with Lola and we still always felt like zombies."

"You know how it is. You do what you have to."

"Yeah." He leaned his head back, stretching out his legs. "What'd you do over the holiday?"

"Moped. With Mom off on a singles' cruise, it just

wasn't the same. She's the one who makes the bulk of the meal."

His hand warming her knee, he said, "Aside from moping, what else did you do?"

"Lisa and I made spaghetti and watched chick flicks." Laughing from the disaster of it, she said, "It was like the anti-Turkey Day. Right down to frozen cheesecake for dessert instead of pumpkin pie." After a moment of silence, she asked, "How about you? Were you with Lola?"

He nodded.

"Well?" she prompted. "How was it? Did you two get any quality time?"

"A little. We went to a dinner and movie. At Dave & Buster's she beat me at Skee-Ball like twenty times in a row."

Laughing, Steph said, "Ouch. That had to wound your male pride."

"A wee bit." He held his thumb and forefinger an inch apart. "But the size of Lola's grin more than made up for my bashed ego. At least we were talking."

"I'm sorry," Stephanie said.

"About what?"

"Everything you're going through," she said. "Loving your kid shouldn't have to be so hard."

"It's not Lola that's the problem. I played a huge role in the person she's become." Growing reflective, he rubbed his whisker-stubbled jaw. "FYI—I took what you said to heart. You know, about me partially to blame for what went down between Vince and Clarissa."

"Oh?" She'd wondered if he'd broach the subject.

"I asked my mom about it. She said I practically invited my brother and wife to have an affair."

"How so?" Shifting her position, she leaned closer to him.

"Working too much. I thought I was doing good by my family, but maybe not."

"I don't buy it," she said, thinking back to the long times she and Michael had spent apart. "Michael was constantly gone. That didn't mean I ran right out to cheat on him."

"Good point." Taking a throw pillow from the end of the sofa, he messed with the fringe. "But to hear Mom talk, you'd think I gave them an engraved invitation to play me for a fool."

"While you were in Seattle, did you talk with Clarissa about it?"

"No." A muscle ticked in his jaw.

"How come?"

"What's the point? When I approached my mom, I was genuinely trying to make sense of it all. You know, what I could've done differently. I admit, I should've spent more time at home, but that doesn't excuse her actions."

"Of course not." Her heart ached for him. But what could she do? "I should never have said you didn't make Clarissa happy."

"Even though it was true?" The hoarseness of his tone revealed his pain. "The crazy thing is," he added with a sad laugh, "in my mind and heart, I really did try making her feel like the most cherished person in my life. That's why I know the whole happily-ever-after routine isn't for me. I tried—and failed miserably."

Chapter Eleven

"Mmm…" Stephanie said early that afternoon, tilting her face back to drink in the sun. The morning's gray skies had been short-lived, and with no wind and temperatures in the midsixties, it had turned out to be a gorgeous day. "This is a treat."

With Brady in town, she'd skipped church, opting instead for a picnic in nearby Roaring Falls National Forest. The girls giggled and shrieked in the infant swings. Brady pushed Michaela while Stephanie pushed Melanie. The fact that Brady got along so well with her girls made her all the sadder for his declaration of being a failure at love.

At this time of year, the park was nearly empty aside from an RV and an orange camper van. What few leaves were still in the trees rustled in the warm breeze.

"This is nice," Brady said. "Just what I needed."

"Glad we could oblige." She winked before giving Melanie another light push. "How long are you staying?"

"Just today. I'm on call Monday, Tuesday and Wednesday, but then I'm off for two days. I thought I'd take Lola up to the mountains. There was an early snow and it's about time she learned to ski."

"Sounds fun," she said, oddly disappointed.

Michaela began to fuss.

"Is that a diaper cry?" Brady asked. "Or her I'm-tired-of-swinging cry?"

"Maybe both," Stephanie said, glad for the distraction.

Sure enough, her firstborn smelled suspicious, so while Steph changed her, Brady took Melanie from her swing to the old quilt they'd spread on a grassy slope.

"Hungry?" After dousing herself in hand sanitizer, Stephanie grabbed the paper sack she'd loaded with ham-and-cheese sandwiches, pretzels and day-old sugar cookies she'd brought home from the shop.

"Always," he said, breaking into a plastic baggie.

"Sorry I couldn't scrounge up anything fancier."

He shrugged. "No sweat. I'm a simple guy. Not really the wine and brie type."

With the babies contentedly gnawing on teething biscuits, Stephanie served herself. "I've never had brie. Is it good?"

Seesawing his hand, he said, "Kind of bland. You haven't missed much."

"I've missed everything." She hadn't meant for the words to slip out, but now that they had, she dove in with a confession. "Michael and I had such plans. After his tour in Iraq, he was going to retire from the military and focus on his work as a commercial pilot. We talked about using his flight privileges to travel the world." With the sleeves of her red sweatshirt, she daubed her stinging eyes.

"Not to sound like an insensitive jerk," he said in a soft, kind tone, "but why can't you still experience your life to the fullest? You're too young to give up."

"I've hardly given up," she snapped, fighting a fresh swell of tears. "Take a look at my reality. In the girls,

I've got a 24/7 job. My hours at the shop aren't much better. I steal maybe an hour or two each night for my self, and that's usually spent doing laundry."

Drawing her into a hug, the sun and the strength of his arms drenching her in hope, she almost dared believe life wouldn't always be so hard.

"You've got to learn to ask for help, Steph."

Shaking her head, she admitted, "I won't be a burden to anyone else."

"Did you ever stop to think that all of your friends— Lisa and Gabby and Olivia—love you? Do you honestly think they consider you a nuisance?"

"I would," she said with a sniffle.

"Bull." Even though he drew back, he still kept hold of her hand. "You're one of the most kindhearted souls I've ever met. What this all comes down to is letting yourself go—not like never washing your hair again, but in releasing your superhuman need for control."

"Control?" That bit of lunacy nearly had her choking on a bite of sandwich. "In case you haven't noticed, I don't have control of much of anything." *Least of all, my feelings for you.*

"Dad, do we have to do this?" Lola complained when Brady headed his Jeep toward the playground at the park near her home. He'd had to scrap their ski trip because of a flu making its way through TransGlobal's pilots. He hadn't been sick, but he was plenty weary of covering for puking crews. "I'm almost nine. Can't we just go to the mall?"

"Your birthday's not until July. And since when do you shop?" he asked, pulling into an empty parking space in front of the swings.

"My friend Becky says only nerds wear clothes not

from the mall. I don't want to be a nerd, so she says I have to go to Abercrombie."

"Since this is the same friend who got you grounded because of her foolproof plan to reunite your mother and me, you might want to ignore her." Turning off the engine, he angled to face his scowling child.

"You don't know anything."

"And you obviously haven't gotten the news that you can't do something just because someone else tells you to. What does your own head say?"

She shrugged.

Hand to his forehead, he sighed.

"What's wrong?"

"Nothing."

"Then how come you're so mad? All I did was ask if we could go to the mall." Her brown eyes sucked him in. He wanted to remain calm and rational, but whenever he was around her, something came up to remind him of just how little he knew his own daughter.

"I'm not mad," he said, thumping the heel of his hand against the wheel. "I'm frustrated. Lola, I miss you. I moved back to Seattle, but we still don't seem to connect. Not the way we used to."

"I miss you, too, Dad, but how are we supposed to be friends when you're flying all the time and when you're not doing that, Mom said Stephanie's your floozy girlfriend and you're shacking up with her."

Hearing that kind of language coming from his innocent child filled him with fury. What the hell was Clarissa thinking?

"What does *floozy* mean?" she asked, pulling down the sun visor presumably to check out her newly straightened hair. "I asked, but she said I was too young to know. But then I got to wondering, if she thinks I'm still a baby, then why was she even saying stuff like that around me?"

"I don't have a clue, but once we get back from the mall, we're going to find out."

Three hours, six shopping bags and two Chick-fil-A combo meals later, Brady pulled the car up to the curb of what used to be his home. Now, it was just a house. The mere sight of the timber and river stone A-frame he'd been so proud of turned his stomach. The views of Puget Sound he'd once found mesmerizing failed to stir him.

"Dad?" Lola asked, taking his hand as they approached the front door. Her uncharacteristic affectionate touch warmed him more than the rare Seattle sun.

"Yes, ma'am?"

"Are you and Mom going to fight? Because if you are, I'm going to my tree house."

A muscle ticking in his jaw, he gave Lola's hand a firm squeeze before saying, "I don't want to fight, but just in case, you might want to call over that neighbor girl you like. What's her name? Lizzie? Loretta?"

"Lauren," she said with a glare. "Why can't you ever remember?"

"Does it matter?"

"Yes." Arms crossed, she stared hard out the passenger-side window.

"I'll try harder, okay?" He gave her hair a tousle.

Flinching, she snapped, "No, you won't. You care about everyone on the planet more than me." Tears slid down her still adorably chubby cheeks.

"That's not true, and you know it." He tried hugging her, but she pushed him away.

"Prove it."

"How?" He'd already moved to Seattle. What more proof did she need?

"Prove you love me more than that Stephanie lady. Mom says she has baby twins. Do you like her more than Mom because her babies are cuter than me?"

Drawing her into a hug, and this time holding on no matter how hard she struggled, he kissed the top of her head. When she finally stopped crying and went limp in his arms, he said, "You're crazy. No baby—or little girl—could ever be cuter than you."

"P-promise?" Her red-eyed sniffles shattered him.

"Absolutely." What was going through Lola's head that she'd even wonder about him loving another kid more than her? "Tell you what, how about the next time I see Steph and her girls, you come along for the ride? Does that sound fun? You like babies, don't you?"

"Y-yeah…I guess." Twirling a lock of her hair, she asked, "They don't smell bad, do they?"

"No. But if they do, I'll bet Steph would let you change their diapers."

"Eeuw!" She pretended to look disgusted, but a hint of a grin and the sparkle in her eyes gave her away. "Can I go with you right now?"

"I don't know about us leaving right this second, but as soon as we clear it with your mom and you have a school break, I'm sure Steph would love having you for a visit."

"YOU'VE ALREADY SUNK LOW enough to sleep with my brother," Brady said under his breath to Clarissa even though Lola was safely out of earshot in the backyard, "but I never imagined you'd stoop to turning my own daughter against me."

"How exactly did I do that?" She slammed a can of

green beans on the counter. She'd been grocery shopping, and was putting them away when he'd brought their daughter home. "Honestly, Brady, you've always been such a drama queen."

Taking a deep breath, he said, "Why'd you tell Lola I'm *shacking up* with a *floozy?* You and Steph used to be friends."

"I never said anything of the sort." Out of a paper bag came boxes of Cheerios, three brands of crackers and the oatmeal pies Lola had loved since she'd first had teeth. "She's been running with a foulmouthed crowd at school. I'm sure one of them said it."

"Cut the B.S., Rissa. Why do you have such a hard time telling the truth?"

"Me?" She snorted. "Don't get me started on how many times you promised to cut back on your precious flight schedule to stay home with me, only to call at the last minute, telling me you weren't coming home. You want to talk lies, Brady, you can damn well start there."

Fighting with everything in him not to match her angry tone, he clenched a fist. "Where do you get off, bitching about my long hours at work, doing everything I could to put you and Lola up in this gorgeous home, when all the time you were screwing my brother behind my back?"

"That's ancient history," she snapped. "Get over it."

Refusing to waste one more minute of his life on senseless arguing with a woman whose only admirable quality had been giving birth to their daughter, he straightened his shoulders. Through gritted teeth, he said, "I have never asked one thing of you. I gave you this house. Your car. Have never been so much as a day late on child support. So over Lola's Christmas break, consider her mine."

"But I always have her over the holidays. What will our families say?"

"I don't give a damn. All I know is that I've wasted years with Lola, and I won't throw away one second more. If you want to fight me on this, I'll be all too happy to sue for joint custody."

"You wouldn't?" She'd gripped a loaf of white bread so tightly that it was now nearly flattened.

"Try me. I'm tired of *always* being the one turning the other cheek. What I'm asking isn't unreasonable. Aside from my few weekends, you and my brother have her the rest of the year."

BY THE TIME BRADY HASHED OUT the details, letting Lola in on the fact that she'd spend the holidays with him in Arkansas, he was not only exhausted, but running late for his return commuter hop to Dallas. Thank God, he wasn't scheduled to fly, or he'd have called in sick.

Once he reached the gate, it was full.

Crying babies. Corporate executives ticking away on their iPhones and BlackBerries. Families bickering over who was to stand watch over the carry-ons while the lucky ones headed out to forage for food. Just a few days earlier, all of this had felt normal. Now, he walked like a stranger through what used to be his home away from home.

He'd expected that having Lola for Christmas would finally banish the gnawing emptiness inside. It helped, but he still didn't feel complete.

Pulling out his cell, he walked a short way to the nearest empty gate before punching in Steph's number.

She answered on the third ring. After exchanging

pleasantries, she asked, "How was your visit with Lola?"

"Better than usual. Which was nice. Even though I've been seeing her more, I only just now learned my little girl religiously uses a hair straightener and shops at mall stores where I'm pretty sure the noise decibels are well over the legal limit."

Laughing, Steph said, "Mmm… Guess I've got that times two to look forward to, huh?"

"Not to mention shelling out an obscene amount of money for what couldn't have been more than a half yard of fabric."

"You're funny. Definitely a daddy who needs more training in the how-to-raise-a-female department."

"Interesting you should say that," he said, pride ringing through his voice. "I just happened to land a pretty major prize that I hope will teach me more about my daughter."

"What happened? Did you reconcile with Clarissa?" Was that concern in her tone? As though his being taken off the market would be a bad thing?

"Not a chance, but Lola's going to spend her entire Christmas break with me, and I'm hoping this isn't presumptuous, but I—*we*—are planning a ski trip, and then we'd like to spend a couple of days with you and your girls. Lola's excited to meet them."

"That's great, but I am going to need details. What are the dates you'll be here? What are her favorite foods? What size does she wear so I can pick up a few gifts. What—"

"Slow down," Brady said with a relieved chuckle. He'd been holding his breath while waiting for her reply. Now that he sensed Stephanie was as excited about his daughter's visit as he was, his heart went out to her a little more. "I've got a full flight schedule for the next three days, but after that—if it's all right with you—I'll stop by so we can make plans."

After saying his goodbyes, Brady tucked his phone in his pocket, leaned his head back and smiled. For the first time since the divorce, he couldn't wait for the holidays.

His argument with Clarissa had flipped a switch in his heart. Though he refused to apologize for working long hours to support his family, he did accept responsibility for not devoting more of his free time to them. Looking back on it, instead of kicking back to watch football and drink beer, he should've taken Lola to the park. Taken Clarissa out for dinner and dancing and movies like they used to before having a baby consumed their lives. He'd dropped the ball. Big-time. And for that, he was sorry. Though it was too late to change the past, from here on out, Lola was getting the absolute best he had to offer.

And Steph? What will you have left to give her?

At the moment, he didn't have a clue.

"Do you think she's having fun?" Stephanie asked, standing alongside Brady at Valley View's ice skating rink. For two weeks every Christmas season, city workers set up an artificially cooled skating pond in the park surrounding the city square. It was most fun when the weather cooperated by staying chilly. But even on years when the temperatures rose into the sixties, it seemed as if the whole town came out to have a good time. Too bad her twins apparently didn't notice, as both girls were snoozing despite blaring Burl Ives and plenty of laughing shrieks when skaters took a dive.

"Duh. Look at the size of her smile."

"Speaking of which, her grin is identical to yours—minus the stubble."

"Let's hope she doesn't inherit my whiskers. My mother's side of the family has some freakishly hairy aunts."

Elbowing him, she said, "Seriously, she's a beautiful girl. When she's not giving me dirty looks, she seems poised for her age. I see why you're so proud."

Eyes welling, he nodded.

"I think you made a good call in staying at a B and B. Less confusion. You know, us being just friends and all."

"Right." His expression darkened. Tone turning serious, he said, "About that…our *friendship*."

Stomach tightening with dread, in a heartbeat her excitement over his visit lessened.

"Hey, whoa," he said with the lopsided grin she adored. Slipping his arm around her shoulders, he kissed her forehead. "I can tell by your pretty pout that you took that the wrong way."

"I'm a grown woman," she was all too happy to point out. "I don't pout."

"If you say so."

Lola came around to their section of the fence. "Look at me, Dad! I'm in the Olympics!" She performed a flawless skip and a hop.

Applauding, Stephanie shouted, "Perfect ten!"

"I say eleven!" Brady chimed in.

Lola waved before heading back out to the skating rink's center where she'd been playing with a group of girls.

"She's adorable," Stephanie said. Kneeling in front of the stroller, she noticed that Michaela had woken from her nap. She wasn't fussy, just wide-eyed at the commotion.

Lifting her from her seat, Stephanie said to her baby girl, "Just think, one of these days, that's going to be you out there."

Michaela didn't look impressed.

"Back to your pouting…" Brady tweaked the baby's nose.

"Oh, whatever." Ignoring him, she hugged her daughter.

"So, like I was saying. After talking with Clarissa, I had an epiphany."

"Uh-huh." Jiggling Michaela, she said, "And I had an early visit from Santa."

"I'm serious." Once smiling eyes turned somber.

"Sorry."

Lola skated around again, hollering at them.

After pasting on a bright smile and waving to the girl, Stephanie asked, "What happened?"

"Clarissa and I had an argument—nothing new. But…" Rubbing his forehead with his thumb and forefinger, he seemed to struggle with what to say next.

With one hand around his back, and her other resting on his abs, she asked, "Everything okay?"

Voice cracking, he said, "Truthfully, I don't know."

"Take it slow," she urged. "One issue at a time."

What was it about her that always made him feel as if no problem was insurmountable? "Everything I thought I knew about what went down between us. In putting the pieces together—little bits from my mom and you, and now Clarissa, for the first time, I'm understanding what role I played in our family falling apart and I don't like the man I see."

"But that was in the past, right? Now, you're doing

everything you can to make things right between Lola and you, and as for Clarissa, it is what it is. She's happy. You can't keep beating yourself up for something irrevocably broken—unless you do want to try winning her back?"

"No." It was the second time Steph had mentioned him patching things up with his ex. Did she honestly think that was a possibility?

"If you wanted to, you probably could…"

How badly he wanted to twine his fingers with Steph's. Maybe in another time, it would've been all right. But for now, he settled for surrendering his pinky finger to Michaela's pinching grip.

"Ouch!" he said in an exaggerated cry. "You're a bruiser."

The baby giggled.

The sound warmed him through and through. Made him want a second chance he didn't deserve. If only he'd done things differently the first time around, maybe he'd still have his own family instead of being on the outside looking in?

With Michaela still in her arms, Stephanie asked, "You look like you just lost your best friend. What gives?"

"Just wondering…"

"Look at *meee!*" Lola called out, whizzing along at top speed.

"About?" Steph adjusted Michaela's red hat to better cover her tiny ears.

"What our lives would have been like if we'd met each other first."

Still fussing over the baby, Steph said, "You mean, if I hadn't met Michael and you hadn't met Clarissa?"

"Yeah." He stared out at the swirl of colorful skaters.

"Suppose I'd still have Lola and you'd still have the girls, but we wouldn't have so much emotional baggage, you know?"

"That would be nice." Gazing up at him, she looked as if she wanted to say more.

"Like the ultimate do-over." In the rink's center, Lola fell, only to hop right up. For a split second, the part of him who would forever worry about her was ready to charge to her rescue. But then she fended for herself, not needing him after all.

"Is that what you're looking for? Redemption in the form of a new family?"

"Absolutely not." *Liar.*

"It wouldn't be the end of the world if you were, you know? Lots of women would be lucky to have you."

But not you?

Chapter Twelve

"Those are kind of cute." Lola frowned at Stephanie's manger-scene cookies. "How did you get all of the faces so perfect?"

"Lots of practice," Stephanie said, piping the edge of the manger.

"Can I try?" the girl asked.

"Sure. Pick out any of the cookies on the racks, and then some frosting." This time of year, Stephanie had piping tubes standing by in a rainbow of colors with all sorts of tips. Though Brady had arranged to take vacation time during Lola's entire school break, a friend's wife had gone into early labor and he needed an emergency replacement. Brady had offered to help by covering a few of his flights. Stephanie loved that about him—that he was willing to give so freely of his time to help a friend in need. Lola, on the other hand, wasn't too thrilled about the idea of Dad being gone.

Though Brady and Lola had been staying at the town's only B and B, during his absence, his daughter was bunking with Steph and her twins.

"The different tips give you different frosting patterns—like this." Using a sheet of wax paper, Stephanie showed Lola an assortment of decorations ranging from petals and basketweaves to hearts and stars. "You try," she said, handing over a tip that made perfect mini Christmas trees that could then be decorated with gold balls and sprinkles.

"This is actually kind of fun," Lola said, sticking out her tongue whenever she concentrated on getting her cookie just right. "Mom's always on a diet, so we don't bake. She says white flour makes her butt big. She does buy me lots of good white stuff, though. She's really, super pretty and I love her lots. She's my best friend in the whole world."

"I'm glad..." Stephanie wasn't surprised that Clarissa was still on a perpetual diet. She'd kept herself in top-notch shape even back when they'd been friends. "I'm sorry your dad had to leave."

"Me, too."

"Sounds like he won't be gone very long."

The little girl actually snorted. "He always says that. I think he leaves all the time because he doesn't want to be with me. Now, he doesn't want to be with you, either."

As much as Lola's words stung, Stephanie was the adult. This was hardly the time to get defensive. Starting a new cookie, she said, "First off, that's totally not true. Your dad adores you. Talks about you all the time. And second, he can't help having a job that makes him go places. It's in his blood."

"Eeuw." Lola made a classic disgusted kid face.

"Not like that," Stephanie said with a laugh. "I mean, that flying is something he *really* loves—kind of like you love mall shopping—only more."

"If he really loved me, he'd stop flying."

"Oh, honey..." Drawing in her lower lip, Stephanie stood a moment to let the full meaning of the girl's statement sink in. When they'd first married, Stephanie remembered having the same thoughts about Michael. About how if he just loved her as much as she loved him, he'd give up flying to be something nice and safe and boring. Gradually, she'd grown to see that flying was as important to Michael as breathing. It wasn't something he merely liked to do, but something he *had* to do. Only now, in retrospect did she get the full gist of what that truly meant. That if Michael had given up his passion for her, he wouldn't have been the same man.

Stephanie explained all of that to Lola, but judging by the girl's blank expression, her words hadn't sunk in.

"Mom said you're a floozy and that you and Dad are shacking up. I asked Dad what *floozy* means, but he wouldn't tell me."

"Oh?" That hurt. Especially since when Stephanie put her mucked up feelings for Brady aside, she still had a soft spot for her old friend. She and Clarissa used to shop together and cook together and, most important of all, commiserate together on the trials of being married to a pilot. "I'm guessing it means that even though they're divorced, your mom might also be having a tough time sharing your father. But I promise, I only want the best for your dad, and that means encouraging him to spend as much time as possible with you."

"Know what I think Mom meant?" Lola asked, the whole of her concentration focused on outlining a cookie manger. "That you're a really nice lady, because being with you is more fun than Girl Scout camp—and that's pretty amazingly fun."

"Thank you." High praise from an eight-year-old. Seeing this new-and-improved soft side to the little girl opened Stephanie's heart to her even more. It was hard enough being married to a pilot, she couldn't imagine the confusion and heartache of having one for a father.

"You're even more fun than Free Fridays at school when we get to raid the craft closet and make anything we want."

"I don't know," Stephanie said, trying to ignore suddenly stinging eyes and a knotted throat. "Making *anything* you want sounds pretty incredible to me."

"It is," Lola said with a grand nod, "but you can't eat friendship bracelets or picture frames." After that observation, she took a huge bite of her latest creation—a pink-and-green reindeer, smiling while she chewed. "So is a floozy like the same thing as a princess or angel? And you never did tell me what's *shacking up?*"

"Steph, I'm sorry." From his bed in the Miami airport Marriott, Brady groaned into the phone. "I never wanted you to find out about that."

"Well, I did," she said, sounding as if she was slamming dishes into the cabinet. "And it was mortifying. I didn't know what to say, so I just stuck with Lola's assumption that a floozy is a good friend and shacking up means that you have slumber parties with ice cream and pizza."

"Damn," Brady said with a whistle. "That's some pretty impressive fibbing."

"Like you did such a great job of explaining? When I asked what you said, she told me nothing, but that your face turned all red and splotchy."

Clearing his throat, he managed, "Red, maybe, but I don't do splotchy."

She laughed.

"Does that mean I'm forgiven?"

"I'll take it under advisement."

He rearranged a pillow to tuck under his neck.

"In the meantime, your daughter is an adorable minx who's interested in everything and has become a talented baker and babysitter."

"She gets along with the twins?"

"Famously. They're inseparable." Her smile rang through her tone, filling him with deep satisfaction. "You should see Lola hauling them around. At first, I was worried, but they laugh and giggle and play epic games of peekaboo."

"Thank you for showing her such a good time." He wished he could give Steph a hug. He missed her. Her sugary scent and laugh and habit of speaking whatever happened to be foremost on her mind.

"It's been my pleasure. I'll be sorry to see her go."

"Is she excited about Christmas?"

"Does Santa carry a few extra pounds around his waist?"

Chuckling, Brady said, "I take it she's driving you nuts with anticipation?"

"Not at all. I love it. It makes me excited for when my girls are old enough to help wrap gifts and decorate the tree."

Closing his eyes, Brady imagined the scene. The twins as chubby toddlers with Lola showing them the ropes. Teaching them all sorts of tricks like searching out their mother's hiding spot for gifts and sneaking bites of holiday sweets before family and guests arrive.

"When are you getting back?" she asked.

"Tomorrow," he said. "And I'm glad. It feels like coming home."

"Y-you'll always be welcome." Was there hesitancy in

her tone? "Everyone should have one place in the world where they feel they best belong."

"But? I sense you're holding back more."

Laughing, she admitted, "You're starting to know me too well."

"So? Out with it."

"I was just going to say that as much as the girls and I love having you here, your true home is with your first family. Lola loves you so much, Brady. Please be careful with her heart. At the moment, she's good, but if you were to do something nutty—say, like spending too much time here and not enough with her—I'm afraid she may never get past the sense of betrayal."

"Betrayal?" He clenched his fists. "You've got to be kidding? So Clarissa marries my brother, has full custody of my kid and lives happily ever after, while I do nothing but dote on Lola for the rest of my life?" Rubbing his suddenly throbbing forehead, he backpedaled. "That came out wrong. It's not that I don't want—and plan—on taking great care of Lola, but is it too selfish to want a little more for me?"

"No, but—"

"When we were at the zoo and Fall Festival and the skating rink, I got this longing to belong to a family—my own family—that struck with enough intensity to actually hurt my chest." He was no doubt crazy for admitting any of that, but it was almost Christmas and he was alone in a hotel room, he was too road-weary to hold anything in. "Sometimes I feel like my whole life has been a screwup. But then I found you again. And since then, I have purpose beyond just treading water with Lola. I'm not sure how or when, but, Steph, I've fallen in love with you. I want to be a real dad to not only her, but your girls. I want a second chance at being a good man for you."

For the longest time, the only sound on the other end of the line was silence. Then muffled sobs. "B-Brady, I'd like that, too, but I can't—won't—be the one who comes between you and your little girl. Not only that, but I'd be crazy to let another pilot into my life. You're a hopelessly nomadic breed who—"

"I get all of that," he said, not in the mood for a play-by-play of why the two of them as a team would never work. It was Christmas, and what he needed was hope. Good, old-fashioned, warm-your-belly *hope*. Not only for a better future, but a better him. "What I want to do is not dwell on all of the reasons why we shouldn't be together—which Lord knows I've done enough of myself, but let's think about how many ways we're right. Think about the insane odds it took for us to even have been on that same flight bound for Miami. Don't you ever get the feeling something's going on behind the scenes? Some force greater than us?"

"I—I want to believe, but if that were truly the case, why did Michael have to die?"

Michael, Michael, Michael. As much as he'd once loved the guy, Brady was now genuinely sick of hearing his name, of constantly being compared to him and in ways, held accountable by his ghost.

Sighing, Brady sliced his fingers through his hair. "When I get back to Valley View, I want the two of us to talk—really talk. In a proper, grown-up setting. We've spent months calling what we share *friendship*, when if both of us were truthful, what we've really been doing is dating."

"No, we're just friends, and—"

He hated cutting her off, but he wasn't in the right

frame of mind for hiding behind labels. "Steph, I don't mean to come off as an insensitive jerk, but face it, something more is simmering between us than mere friendship. We owe it to ourselves to figure out what."

More silence.

"Steph? You there?"

"Brady, I—I'm not sure if I'm emotionally up for—"

"One real date." His pulse took off at a runaway pace. "That's all I'm asking. Think your sister would babysit?"

"My warning alarm's shrieking," Lisa said, holding open her condo's front door while Stephanie handled the bundled up twins in their carriers. Having volunteered to carry the diaper bag, Lola brought up the rear. The night was brutal. Clear, but cold.

Lisa's favorite show, *Project Runway,* blared on her TV.

"Do you always have to be such a downer?" Steph asked low enough that Lola hopefully wouldn't hear. Setting the carriers on the tile entry, she closed the door and took off her coat.

"Cool!" Before Stephanie could even introduce Lola to her sister, she'd dumped the diaper bag and charged off to inspect Lisa's prized saltwater fish tank that she kept in the kitchen.

"Auntie Lisa is not a downer," Stephanie's twin crooned to the grinning girls. "She just worries about your mommy getting her heart broken into a million, cajillion pieces." Tickling tummies until both girls shrieked, she added, "Broken hearts aren't any fun, are they?" Lisa stood, a serious look on her face. "The last thing I want is to fight, but I'm just looking out for you.

Tell me you know what you're doing, and I'll butt out. Promise." She crossed her heart.

"Of course, I know what I'm doing," Stephanie lied. She was in the dark as to where she and Brady stood.

"I hope so." Lisa took Michaela from her. "For the sake of these two cuties, I really, really hope so."

Lola finally wandered into the living room. "Whoa! You two look exactly the same! It's freaky. But still cool."

Lisa laughed, extending her hand for the girl to shake. "I think we're going to get along just fine. I'm Lisa, and I'm assuming you're Lola?"

The girl nodded. "Got any other cool pets?"

"Depends," Lisa said, a touch of mystery to her voice. "Do you like really big birds?"

"Uh-huh." Lisa had a sun conure named Ralph that she housed in front of the bay window in her home office. Judging by the size of Lola's eyes, the girl was expecting a pterodactyl.

Grabbing hold of Lola's hand, Lisa said, "Come with me..." Over her shoulder, she called, "Steph, get out of here. We've obviously got lots to do."

"Bye, Steph!"

Suddenly choked up, Stephanie ran over to Brady's daughter to give her a quick hug. "We won't be back too late, okay?"

"I'm fine," she assured. "I just wanna see the big bird."

"SOUNDS LIKE MY DAUGHTER," Brady said, finishing off a bottle of Merlot into Stephanie's glass after she'd told him of Lola's latest adventure, "she always has wanted to be a zookeeper. Lisa doesn't have any animals I should be worried about, does she?"

"She supposedly has a black cat, but I've never seen it." Stephanie laughed, and in the process, unwittingly tightened his stomach with how pretty she looked by candlelight with Dean Martin in the background, crooning about love. Even though it was barely past nine, their corner table was secluded.

Brady had gotten an earlier flight than he'd expected, and for their first official date had invited her to try a swanky new Italian place that'd opened in Little Rock. The walls were black, as were the upholstered chairs and hardwood floor. Crystal chandeliers provided just enough overhead light to see the meal offerings without being obtrusive. Framed black-and-white landscapes of Venice graced the walls while the only shots of color were plush yellow draperies, cloth napkins and the menus. As eager as he'd been to try the place with Steph, suddenly the lasagna he'd been craving didn't sound nearly as tempting as a taste of her lips.

"I like your dress," he said, "the blue does good things to your eyes."

"Thanks—" she sipped her wine "—you're looking good, too. This is the first time I've seen you in a suit." Having flown into Little Rock on a commercial flight, he'd stopped off for a quick shower and fresh clothes at the B and B where he and Lola would again be staying.

"So what's going on, Brady? Why this sudden change in plans?"

"Damn." He fortified himself with another swig of wine. "Gotta love a woman not afraid to speak her mind."

"You know what I mean."

"I do." And in answer to her question, he was stumped. The words that had come so easily on the phone now seemed stuck at the back of his throat. "Bottom line, I'm tired of our so-called plans. I'm tired of pretending you're just my friend when I still dream of our kiss on the beach."

Ducking her gaze, she developed a sudden interest in the bottom of her wineglass.

"Don't even try denying you think about it, too."

"Yes, but—" She added fanning herself to her avoidance tactics. "That was a long time ago and you're a pilot and I've already been down that road. And then there's Lola and we're just friends, and can you even imagine how upset she'd be to find out we actually are dating?"

Why, he couldn't say, but the thought of tackling her list of insurmountable problems suddenly seemed like the best challenge ever. "What if we worked through all of that?"

"How?" she practically shrieked.

The couple four tables over stopped their conversation to stare.

Covering her mouth, Steph mumbled, "Sorry. Maybe I need more wine and I'll see all of this as easily as you."

He wagged the bottle. "That can be arranged."

She laughed, and her smile filled him near bursting with sensations he hadn't felt since college. Like excitement over just being with her. He found himself wanting to do anything within his power to make her happy.

"You're awful," she said, still chuckling.

"You're just now figuring that out?" he asked more quietly than he would've liked. What was he doing? All of this had been simple when they'd only been old friends. With each visit, it was growing harder to pretend he didn't care.

Reaching across the table, he took her hands, brushing the pads of his thumbs against her palms. "Aside from my daughter, I can't remember what I used to spend my time on before meeting you."

"I know," she admitted, seeming a little short of breath. Was she feeling as much confusion as him about where this *friendship* was headed? "I find myself thinking about you more and more. When you're not here, I wonder where you are." Licking her lips, she added, "I wonder, too, if you're thinking about me."

Forcing air into his lungs, he didn't know where to start. She was a single mom. Last thing he wanted was to lead her on. But then who was he fooling? He had every bit as much to lose by falling for her as she did him. What would Lola say? He had a tough enough time talking with her on his own—throw in a stepmom and two siblings? Talk about a recipe for disaster. Trouble was, Stephanie expected—and deserved—no less than marriage, and that was the one thing he wasn't capable of giving. Knowing that, was it even fair for him to be here with her?

"Guilty," he confessed, ignoring the voice of reason in his head. "I do think about you—a lot."

Her smile brightened her blue eyes. "That's good, because this wine has me thinking I might just want to try kissing you again." Giggling, she covered her mouth. "Did I really just say that?"

He nodded. Was it a problem he wanted to kiss her, too?

"More wine?" their waiter stopped by to ask.

"We're fine," Brady said. He didn't think it was right to loosen Stephanie's inhibitions even more than he already had.

"I would've liked a teensy bit more," she complained

once the waiter had left. She'd already finished the glass he'd just poured her.

"I know, and I'm sorry to cut you off," he reasoned, "but we do need to pick up the girls."

"Later..." Her pretty pout was nearly his undoing. How easy it would be to bundle her into the car, drive to her house, and then give her exactly what she—what they both—wanted.

Easy. But not very honorable.

The jury still out on which way the night would go, he signaled the waiter for the bill.

"Oh, we're leaving?" Trying to get her arms into her coat sleeves while still seated proved no easy feat.

"Let me help," he said, trying to resist the urge to take her in his arms. She smelled of the pastry shop. Of homemade goodness. Cinnamon and sugar. Nutmeg and vanilla.

When the waiter finally came back, Brady handed over his Visa without looking at the meal's total.

"Don't pay yet," Steph said, "I need more wine."

"I know," he assured, slipping his arm around her for their walk to the front door. "Next time we go out, we'll order lots more."

"Mmm..." She snuggled against him. "That sounds fun."

She had no idea....

By the time they reached her house, she'd fallen asleep. He hated rousing her, but he needed the key.

Once inside the dark living room, she turned and stood on her tiptoes to slide her arms around his neck. "Finally, I get to kiss you." Before he had time to stop her, she'd pressed her lips to his, unleashing an erotic bolt for which he'd had no time to prepare.

Softly moaning, she sighed open her lips, inviting him in. And he went willingly.

"Um," he said, pulling back reluctantly and with a voice husky with the exquisite pain of a hard-on he feared would be with him the remainder of the evening. After flicking on the overhead lights, he said, "We should probably get you to bed."

"I like that idea." The twinkle in her eyes told him she had no intention of sleeping. Lucky for him, he knew that with her being such a lightweight, she'd conk out the second her head hit the pillow.

Scooping her into his arms, he carried her down the hall, stopping along the way to flip on the light with his elbow.

In her moonlit room, he set her on her bed, tugging off her coat and shoes.

"I can do it," she argued, trying to sneak another kiss while he pulled back her covers.

"I know you can. I just thought you might like help."

Sighing into her pillow, the sweetest smile curving her lips, she murmured, "Help's nice. Doing everything by myself is getting old."

"I know," he said, pressing a chaste kiss to her forehead. On her nightstand were a series of silver-framed pictures featuring her husband. A formal shot of him in uniform. A candid wedding photo of her grinning while he fished for her garter. A casual snapshot of her sitting on his lap, kissing his cheek at what looked to be a boisterous family picnic.

"This is nice," he said, pointing to the last pic. "Is this Michael's family?"

She nodded. "They're all from Michigan. That was taken at their lake house the summer before..."

"Sorry," Brady said. "I didn't mean to bring you down."

"It's okay," she said, her voice childlike as she snuggled into her pillow. "I thought they would visit more to see the girls, but after Michael died, his mom fell apart. That day feels like a dream. Like it never even happened...."

When she closed her eyes, Brady was shamefully relieved. He didn't feel qualified to even comment on how painful losing her husband must've been.

He sat on the edge of the bed, swiping his hands through his hair. What had he done? In kissing Steph again, he'd opened a Pandora's box he wasn't sure how—or, even if he wanted—to close. Their date had been his idea, but faced with all of her reminders of Michael, Brady was starting to feel like Steph's consolation prize. Hell, yeah, he wanted her in every way a man could, but he also wanted self-respect. Before taking things further, he needed her promise that she wasn't just using him as a stand-in for the man she truly wanted.

Chapter Thirteen

"Having fun?" Brady asked Lola late Christmas morning. She sat cross-legged in front of the crackling fire with the twins as her audience. Though Stephanie's house wasn't anywhere near as *fancy* as the one in which Lola had grown up, she looked content putting on a show with her new Barbie dolls, animatedly telling Melanie and Michaela the proper way to brush hair.

"Yup," she said, flashing him a huge smile. "I like having little sisters. I've never been this close to babies before. They're mini-people. Only they can't do anything but pee and poo and burp and stuff. But they're still cool. I wish I could keep them."

"They'd probably miss their mom." He sat on the brick hearth, stroking her long brown hair.

"I know. And if I stayed here, I'd miss my mom, but my friend Becky has two moms, and she really loves both."

Michaela grabbed a Barbie shoe and crammed it in her mouth.

"No!" Lola took it from her. "Bad baby. You can't eat high heels, or they'll give you a stomachache." Rolling her eyes, she said to Brady, "It's very hard work watching them all the time."

"I'll bet." It was funny how back in Seattle, Lola

seemed in so many ways as if she was growing up too fast. Yet since being here, she'd reverted back to his sweet little girl. "Would you like having two moms?"

"Sure. If I got to see you more. I like Uncle Vince, but you're my favorite."

Was it wrong that her declaration made him happy?

"What are you two up to?" Stephanie strolled in from the kitchen, wiping her hands on a lacy white apron. She'd been cooking up a storm in anticipation of her sister's visit. Cakes and a ham and all of the trimmings.

Standing, hands on her hips, Lola said, "I've been trying to teach the babies how to be beauty parlor ladies, but they keep eating all of the brushes."

"Thank you for taking such good care of them," Stephanie said. "Want your dad to take over so you can help me in the kitchen?"

"I'd like to," she said, "but Dad's not as good as me at teaching babies."

"Hey," Brady protested, "I did all right with you, didn't I?"

"Come on," Stephanie said, holding out her hand to his daughter. "I need help mashing the potatoes."

"That sounds fun," Lola said, abandoning her dolls and wide-eyed pupils to play in the kitchen instead.

Seeing Lola hand in hand with the woman who'd grown to mean so much did strange things to Brady's heart. His late-night worries over Steph still being hung up on Michael now seemed stupid.

"OKAY, SO HE'S CUTE, charming and funny, and Lola's a doll," Lisa whispered, having dragged Steph into the nursery while her current boyfriend, Kent, and Brady cleaned up after dinner. The babies had long since been tucked into their cribs and Lola had crashed on the living-room sofa while valiantly trying to stay awake through her new Disney DVD. "So what's the catch? Something's got to be wrong with him."

"Nope. Perfect through and through."

"Now I know something's up." Hand beneath Stephanie's chin, she said, "You're glowing. Everything in me is screaming to watch out for you, but maybe I'm wrong, and for once you do know what you're doing."

"For once?" Cocking an eyebrow, Stephanie asked, "So if I'm such a loser when it comes to love, how come I've only been with two men, while—"

"You and Brady have…" Waving her hand, Lisa said, "…*you know?*"

Lips pressed into a stern line, Stephanie said, "Not that it's any of your business, but no, Brady and I haven't made love. But when we do, it's going to be amazing." If their kisses had been anything to judge by, being wholly with him would be extraordinary. How blessed she was to have found him. "So what's up with you and Kent?"

"I don't know. He's okay, but definitely not marriage material."

"Then why are you with him?"

"He's fun. I'm not ready to settle down." Folding a tiny T-shirt Stephanie had left in a basket on the chair, she said, "Sometimes I think you were born married."

"What if I was?" Stephanie folded towels.

Leaning against the doorjamb, twirling her hair, Lisa said, "Lola's a cutie. The spitting image of her dad."

"She told me her mom called me a floozy."

"Ouch." Lisa gave her a hug. "Want me to tear her hair out for you?"

Half-smiling, Stephanie said, "Sounds like a plan."

"Speaking of which, what happens if you and Brady get serious? You prepared to take on another child?"

Without hesitation, Stephanie surprised even herself by saying, "Yes."

"IT'S BEEN A PERFECT DAY." After saying goodbye to Lisa and Kent, Brady met Stephanie alongside the glowing Christmas tree. He wrapped his arms around her waist. "Thank you."

"My pleasure." She returned his hug. Looking to Lola, who was still passed out on the sofa, she asked, "Want to stay here tonight? I'd hate to wake her."

"Sounds nice. It's cold outside."

"Let me warm you," she teased, running her hands up his back. Her touch felt so good. Like much-needed balm.

"I almost forgot. I have one more present for you."

"Mmm...I like gifts. Is it big or small?"

Wrinkling her nose, she said on her way to the hall closet, "Sort of in-between. And before you get too excited, it's not that big of a deal. Just something I snagged in an online auction that I thought you might like to have."

"I'm intrigued." He followed her, admiring her walk. The way her hips gently swayed. She had a lushness about her that had him constantly wanting to touch.

"You should be," she said with a hint of sass while presenting him with a sky-blue gift-wrapped box. "It's not every day you get a present like this. Come on." Taking him by the hand, she drew him into her room, shutting the door.

"I'm liking this already," he said in his best bad-boy tone.

Landing a light smack to his chest, she told him to behave before sitting on the rumpled bed. "Well? Aren't you going to open it?"

"Nothing personal, but I'm kind of enjoying myself just standing here, looking at you."

She flushed and looked down.

"What? Don't believe me?" Joining her on the bed, he cupped her cheeks, brushing her lower lip with his thumb. He kissed her. Slow and sweet, with all of the wanting he'd held in for so long. She tasted of pecan pie and hot chocolate with mint. Of the dream he'd secretly carried of finding someone who cared for him the way he cared for others.

He might've started the kiss, but she deepened it, making him crazy with soft mews.

Her tongue stroking his was his undoing.

Easing her back on the bed, he set her present aside, choosing instead to take her as his gift. Moonlight cast her in an ethereal glow, transforming her winter-pale skin and wild curls into the stuff of dreams. Kissing her throat, her collarbone, only made him want more. Undoing the buttons on her chaste, green silk blouse revealed a red scrap of a bra complete with rhinestones and sequins.

"Ho, ho, ho," he teased, hard as a freaking rock. "Did you plan to seduce me?"

"Maybe." Licking her lips, she admitted, "I know I've thought a lot about it."

"Sure this is what you want?" he asked, skimming his hand along her bare abdomen.

She nodded.

"I don't have a condom."

Laughing, she said, "Wow. Hadn't even thought of that. I sure don't have one."

"Talk about putting on the brakes." Sitting back on his haunches, he swiped his fingers through his hair. "I feel like I'm in one of those old Road Runner cartoons, and just got blown to bits by TNT."

"It'll be okay," she said, tugging him back down.

For the first time in his life, he didn't give a damn about the consequences. Hell, he didn't think for a second she had any disease, meaning the worst that could happen was them making a baby. As much as she'd come to mean to him, he was all for it.

"I want you," he said, burying his face in her hair.

"Then what's stopping us?"

"Truth?" He glanced at her nightstand. At her shrine to her late husband. "Honor. You told me Michael gave you his blessing to start a new life, but he wouldn't want you sleeping around without a commitment."

"So?" Resting on her elbows, her breasts straining at the red satin bra, she said, "What are you waiting for? Make an honest woman of me."

Taken aback by her suggestion, it took a second for her words to even sink in. By then, he'd stood, working off excess energy by pacing the room. "L-like in marriage? You seriously feel you're over Michael and would want to marry me?"

"Duh. You literally saved my life. Before meeting you, every day was a struggle. Now, they're a gift. You've not only transformed me, but everything I thought to be true."

Forehead furrowed, he said, "I don't even know what that means."

"Simple." Stepping up behind him, she said, "When Michael died, I thought my life was over. I want to repay the favor by turning right back around to rescue you. I know it sounds crazy and we're probably rushing into something best given more thought, but I don't care. Lisa's all the time worrying about me but for once, I'm doing what my heart says instead of my head. Marry me, Brady. You mean everything to me, and I want to mean the same to you."

"You already do." Spinning to face her, he kissed her long and hard. And when he'd finally had his fill, he scooped her into his arms, carrying her back to the bed. Making love to her in the sweetest way he knew.

Good morning, sleepyhead."

Stephanie was slow to wake, only to find herself using Brady's shoulder for a pillow. "I thought last night had been a dream."

"Oh—it was. Those red satin panties are forever burned into my brain."

"Is that a good thing?" she asked with a shy smile.

He answered with a kiss. "A *very* good thing."

From behind the closed bedroom door came double wails. "That, on the other hand," he said, easing out from under her with a good-natured groan, "sounds like a not-so-good thing."

"I never sleep this late," she said, covering a yawn while pulling the sheet over her bare breasts. She also wasn't in the habit of waking up next to a naked man! "The girls are probably starving. All three of them."

"Should we make breakfast or go out?" Because Stephanie had closed her shop for two days after Christmas, she had time for either.

"We've got so many leftovers," the thrifty side of her pointed out, "we should probably stay home."

"There's our answer." He pulled on the jeans he'd abandoned on the floor. Remembering that moment made her hot all over—not to mention the sight of his well-toned derriere. "Going out it is. You exhausted me last night, and I could use a waffle."

"Brady! You shouldn't say things like that."

"Waffle?" After leaning down to grace her with a kiss that told her in no uncertain terms how much he cared, he winked. "I've always liked that word. Now, let me get the munchkins rounded up, and you grab a quick shower or do whatever mysterious things women have to do to get out of the house in a hurry."

An hour later, seated at the insanely crowded IHOP out by the highway, Stephanie felt as if she were living a dream. With her two girls in high chairs, gobbing at pieces of blueberry pancakes—without sticky syrup— and Lola seated alongside her with a platter of what looked to be more whipped cream than pancake extravaganza, she felt inordinately blessed. Glancing up to see Brady seated across from her, flashing his most sexy grin, threw her over the top.

Refusing to cry on such a happy day, she asked, "Feeling brave enough to drive into Little Rock to hit a mall?"

"Yeah!" Lola cried. "I *love* the mall."

With a good-natured groan, Brady said, "Guess I'd better get used to being outnumbered, huh?"

"Looks that way," Stephanie said, "unless you're having second thoughts?"

"Not a one." Under his breath for only her to hear, he added, "I can't wait to marry you."

Her giant kid ears working overtime, Lola asked, "What're you whispering about, Dad?"

"I was going to wait to tell you, but now seems as good a time as any." Taking his daughter's hand, and then Stephanie's, he said, "Last night, after you conked out on the sofa, Stephanie and I had a grown-up talk, and—"

"Did you kiss?" the girl asked with her loaded fork to smiling lips.

Reddening, Brady cleared his throat. "Maybe once, but the main thing we did was make what I think is a pretty great decision that also involves you."

"Like what?" The girl's smile faded. "You're not moving even further away, are you?"

"Not a chance. I asked Stephanie to marry us. And she said, yes."

"That's a relief." Blowing out a gush of air, Lola's grin grew to epic proportions. "I thought you were moving to *Mongolinoa,* or something. But if you're just getting married, then we have lots to do."

"Really?" he asked, "like what?"

"Well…I don't know how Stephanie said she'd marry you without a ring, Dad, but while we get a cake and flowers and a white horse for me and her to ride down the aisle, you have to get her a *super* big gigantic diamond."

"I DON'T NEED THIS TO MARRY you," Stephanie protested at a glitzy mall jewelry store. The size of the rock he'd slipped onto her finger was obscene. Gorgeous. But way too big. Even if it did sparkle like rainbows and fairy dust and make her feel like a princess being swept off to a castle.

"Yes, you do," Lola said from her post behind the twins' stroller. "My friend Becky said her mom won't marry anyone who gives her a crappy ring. It's the most important start to any relationship."

Scowling, Brady asked, "Remember the talk we had about you not listening to everything Becky says?"

"Yeah," Lola said with a big nod, "but it's okay this time, 'cause she knows everything about love."

Lips still pressed into a stern line, he said, "We'll discuss that later."

"Is this the one you'd like?" the salesclerk asked. Her gray eyes shone almost as brightly as the stone. No doubt the college-aged girl stood to gain a hefty commission.

"It's beautiful," Stephanie said, "but too much. Let's look at smaller diamonds."

"She wants that big square one, Dad."

"I agree," Brady said. To the clerk, he added, "Could I please have it gift wrapped?"

"Absolutely." She held out her hand to Stephanie. "Ma'am? The ring?"

"I have to give it back?"

"Yes," Lola and her dad said at the same time.

"Dad has to ask you to marry him better now that he has a ring. Like he'll rent a football stadium or stick the ring in cake, or maybe even hire ballerinas to swirl around and—"

"Whoa," he said to their self-appointed wedding planner with a ruffle to her hair. "Slow down. I'm not really the fancy proposal type."

"You better start." Hands on her hips, Lola noted, "If you don't ask Stephanie in a *really* super great way, she'll say no, and then we won't get any more of her cookies."

"In that case," he teased while Stephanie handed over her ring, "I might need to step up my game, because I *really* like Steph's cookies."

His loaded double entendre earned him a swat from the bride-to-be.

THAT NIGHT, AFTER ALL of the girls had crashed—
Lola on a comfy pallet in the twins' room, since they
were having a sleepover—Brady finally got Stephanie
to himself.

"It's been a long day," he said, snagging her around
her waist to draw her onto his lap. He sat on the sofa, the
only light coming from the Christmas tree and glowing
fire. "Tired?"

She nodded. "But in a good way. Lola's awesome. I
don't know what you've been worried about. She adores
you."

"The feeling's mutual. I'm just worried that once she
returns to Seattle, everything will go back to the way
it was. You know, with her constantly being sassy, and
giving me lots of angsty, preteen looks."

"She'll be fine," Stephanie assured. "And I was thinking, what if you filed for joint custody? It might be best
if she stays in school in Seattle, but how amazing would
it be if she spent her summers with us?"

"Have I mentioned how great you are?" Throat swell-
ing with emotion, he had a tough time believing how
sudden all of this had come about, but at the same time,
how right it felt. As if he and Stephanie had been meant
to find each other.

"Not lately," she teased, "but I'm always happy to
hear all about it."

He kissed the tip of her cute, perky nose. "Then
you're in luck, because every day we're together, I'm
going to ramble on and—"

She hushed him by pressing her lips to his. "Rather
than discussing the glory that is me, I'd much rather
make this dream official. Where's my ring?"

He burst out laughing. "That's my girl. Always a
straight shooter."

"It's your fault," she rationalized. "If you hadn't bought me such a gorgeous bauble, I wouldn't want to be wearing it."

"Okay," he said, taking her tiny, gift-wrapped box out from behind a sofa cushion where he'd hidden it for this very occasion, "but for my sake, please spin a fabulous yarn about how I asked you to marry me in the most romantic way ever."

"Wait," she said, feigning a pout. "You mean, you're just going to straight out ask me, and then stick a ring on my finger?" She shook her head. "That will never do."

Growling, he nuzzled her neck. "How about I tell you how much I love you, we share a repeat performance of last night, and then I put your ring on your finger?"

All smiles, she said, "Works for me."

Long after they'd made love and his perfect fiancée had drifted off to sleep wearing her ring, Brady stared at the ceiling, wondering what he'd done right to deserve so much happiness.

How lucky he was that Lola had even fallen in love with Steph. And he knew he loved Steph, too. At first, he'd worried it was the excitement of the proposal that had his pulse racing and mouth dry, but then he'd seen the depth of his feelings reflected back to him in Steph's big blue eyes. From that moment on, he knew he'd never again doubt they were making the right decision. Yes, it was hasty. Yes, they should probably wait to marry. But did he want to? Hell, no.

How often in life was a man given the ultimate do-over? His first marriage might've gone horribly wrong, but this time, he was going to get everything right.

Sounded convincing, so why, when Brady rolled over to find himself facing Michael's pictures, did his gnawing stomach not seem so sure?

Chapter Fourteen

"Good Lord," Gabby said upon admiring Stephanie's engagement ring. While Brady had taken the girls to the Little Rock Zoo, Stephanie indulged in a playdate with her favorite big girls. They all shared a roomy corner booth at Senor Fajitas, enjoying a pitcher of margaritas and plenty of chips and salsa. "This guy must seriously like you."

"I hope so," she quipped, "because I seriously like him."

"Yeah, but don't you think this is moving too fast?" Lisa dredged a chip into the *queso* they'd also ordered. "You hardly know the guy. When we talked on Christmas, I knew you two were officially dating, but how did you get from your first date to marriage in a night?"

"Do you always have to be such a downer?" Stephanie snapped. "For once in a long time, I'm happy. What's wrong with you that you can't celebrate with me?"

"Oh—" Lisa said with plenty of attitude "—if I thought for one minute you knew what you were doing, I'd support you all the way, but you seem to have forgotten that just a couple of months ago you suffered from panic attacks. One so severe it nearly landed you in jail. What happened to them? Since meeting Brady, you've stopped going to your doctor and seem to spend your days skipping around like—like I don't know, some perpetually high sugarplum fairy."

Hand on Lisa's forearm, Olivia said, "How about toning it down a notch. Steph's got a great head on her shoulders and if she likes Brady, I'm sure he's a truly wonderful guy. He has a great job, loves and supports his daughter, and is prepared to do the same for Steph's girls."

Gabby piped in with, "I, for one, couldn't be happier for you, sweetie. Though I'm miffed about still not having met the man, I'm sure I'll love him just as much as you."

A lump in her throat the size of a small house, Stephanie nodded, profoundly grateful for her friends' support when her own twin seemed hell-bent on canceling the wedding before it even happened.

"Let's toast," Olivia said, raising her margarita glass, "to Steph and her girls. May you all live happily ever after."

While everyone else shared glass-clinks and smiles, Lisa sat with her arms tightly folded. Her expression unmistakably read that she thought Stephanie was making a huge mistake. But from Steph's point of view, the only cloud hanging over her future marriage was her poor choice in her maid of honor.

"I HATE GOODBYES," STEPHANIE said two days later when Brady had his car loaded up to head back to the airport. He'd hoped to spend New Year's with her, but flu was again making the rounds, and he'd been called back in to work. Lola had wanted to stay with Steph, but logistically, he couldn't work out getting her back to Seattle in time for school.

"Me, too," he said, wrapping her in a bear hug, "but

I'll be back soon, and we can start fighting over wedding cake flavors."

Smiling through silent tears, she nodded, leaving him to hug his daughter. "I'm going to miss you, Lola. You're an awful lot of fun."

"I'm gonna miss you, too," Lola said, "but when I come back for our wedding, we're gonna have the best time ever."

"Absolutely," Stephanie said with a firm nod.

While Lola fussed over the twins, who sat in their stroller, Brady took Steph's hands, giving them a squeeze. "Hey, don't be so glum. I'll be back before you know it."

"I know," she said, freeing one hand to swipe more tears. "I'm being silly, blubbering like this."

"It's not silly, but sweet. Endearing. But you have to know I hate seeing you cry—especially over a lug like me."

She nodded.

"You going to be all right?"

"Yes," she managed through a grin. "Just get out of here before I make an even bigger scene."

He gave her and the twins one last kiss and hug before climbing behind the wheel.

Now, Lola was crying, too. "I love you," she said as she wrapped her arms around Stephanie's waist.

"Love you, too." Kissing the crown of Lola's head, Stephanie patted her behind to get in the car. "I'll see you real soon. And don't forget to e-mail me. I want to know how Becky likes all of your new clothes."

"Okay," Lola promised.

With one last wave, Brady turned the ignition and backed his rental car out of the drive. Seeing all of his girls teary-eyed had him choked up, as well.

"I sure like them," Lola said. Fat tears lined her cheeks and at the first stop sign, Brady pulled her into a hug.

"They're pretty great, huh?"

She nodded. "Do you think Mom's gonna be mad at me for liking Stephanie, too?"

"No way," he instinctively said while making a left out of Steph's neighborhood. Along with a fresh start with Steph, he figured it was about time he forgave Vince and gave him his blessing on helping to raise Lola. "I'm sure she'll be happy that you're happy."

"Yeah."

"You don't sound so sure." He glanced her way. She'd opened her pink Barbie purse and took out a fluffy, pink ball gown.

"I know. It's just that sometimes when I talk about you, Mom doesn't like it. She doesn't say bad stuff about you, or anything, but she acts like she'd be happiest if you went away."

Nice.

"I'm sure she doesn't mean it like that," he covered while secretly believing his ex would like nothing better than for him to fall off the planet.

"I guess. But, anyway, she always likes getting new dresses, so she'll be glad about that."

"What do you mean?" Brady asked, merging the car onto the highway.

"Don't you think she'll want a fancy dress to wear to the wedding?" With an excited squirm, she added, "Maybe me and her can even be flower girls together!"

"Sure this is the one?" Olivia asked Stephanie on a blustery January Saturday morning. They'd been shopping for wedding dresses for two weeks with no luck, yet in Little Rock's Bridal Emporium, the first white satin gown she'd slipped on fit like a dream.

"Look at it," Stephanie said, admiring herself in a three-way mirror. Thanks in part to an angry sky threatening snow, aside from a lone sales attendant they had the place to themselves. "It's got the sweetheart neckline I like, tons of beading on the bodice, a full, tulle skirt—even the eighty million buttons I wanted in the back."

"You do know you'll have to pay me extra for helping with all of those?" Olivia teased.

"Fair enough." Since her falling out with Lisa, Stephanie had asked Olivia and Gabby to be co-matrons of honor. On this day, Gabby was unfortunately with Dane at a Vegas legal conference. They'd had a good laugh about hundreds of judges meeting up in Sin City. Brady was home watching football with the twins, who were all of the sudden walking like crazy, and refused to be in their stroller a second longer than necessary. "What kind of veil should I wear?"

"Honestly, with all of your gorgeous curls, I'd wear your hair down and wild, letting it be your veil. For extra pizzazz, you can top it off with a tiara."

"Ooh, that sounds cute. What about shoes?"

After a moment of surveying the dress, Olivia said, "If you want to go all out, I'd say matching satin pumps. But knowing your aversion to heels, how about we get you a fancy pair of sneakers? You know, the ones with all the beading and lace. Your skirt is so full, no one will see them but you, and you'll be a lot more comfortable at the reception."

"You always give the best advice." Hopping down from the alterations podium, she gave her friend a hug.

"Thank you. For not just putting up with my endless dress shopping, but helping me deal with Lisa. She's really putting a damper on my fun."

"Don't let her get to you," Olivia said, fluffing Stephanie's hair. "She'll eventually come around, and when she does, she'll give you a big apology and everything will be better between you."

"Hope so." Staring at herself in the mirror, Stephanie suddenly felt old. Tired. She'd been through a lot for such a young age. It seemed as if only yesterday since she'd been dress shopping for her wedding to Michael. Her budget had been much smaller, and she'd ended up having a friend's mother make her gown. It'd been simple, yet elegant. Perfect for their summer garden wedding.

Eyes closed, she saw Michael standing at the end of the morning glory-covered gazebo that'd served as their altar. He'd worn his navy dress whites. His white rose boutonniere matched the flowers in her hair.

Lightning bugs glittered like stars in the trees and the perfection of the moment they shared their first kiss as man and wife had been spellbinding.

From out of nowhere, her heart began to race.

Eyes open, she said to Olivia, "I have to get out of this dress."

"What's wrong?" her friend asked. "Are you sick?"

Unable to speak, Stephanie just nodded.

Clawing frantically at the row of buttons she'd once thought charming, she felt light-headed and queasy and drenched with sweat. "I have to get out. Please, help me."

"I am," Olivia assured, "but just like it took a while to get you into this fancy number, it's going to take time to get you out."

"No," Stephanie said with a wild shake of her head. "I need air. I can't breathe. Seriously, I'm going to die." Bolting from the dressing room with her dress only half-undone, she found an emergency back exit that when she pressed the panic bar, launched a fire alarm's wail.

The clerk came running. "Is everything all right?"

Outside, sleet pelted Stephanie's bare arms and face. She didn't care. She was beyond caring. All she knew was that she had to run as far as possible to escape. To find her way back to Michael. But she was so tired, and her limbs ached. She tried reaching Olivia's SUV, but her legs turned numb, buckling with her every step.

"She can't wear that dress out of here," the clerk shouted. "It's over three thousand dollars."

"Leave us alone for a second," Stephanie heard Olivia tell the woman, "and I promise we'll be right in to pay."

"Do I have *stupid* written on my forehead? Your crazy friend just set off my fire alarm, and now she's out in the snow, wearing one of my priciest gowns."

"Oh, for heaven's sake," Olivia snapped, digging through her purse and then flinging her Visa Platinum across the pavement. "We're paying for the damned dress. Just leave us alone."

With an indignant string of insults, the woman finally left.

"Steph? Honey?" Olivia slowly approached. "Where's your medication?"

"I don't know," she said through messy tears. "I don't have attacks anymore, so I didn't think I'd need it."

"Uh-huh." With so much of her skin exposed, in the midteen temperatures, Stephanie's teeth began to chatter. Olivia wrapped her arms around her, urging her back into the shop. "Come on, honey. Let's get you warmed up."

Exhausted, Stephanie went along with whatever

Olivia wanted her to do. She usually insisted on making her own decisions, but with Michael's heartbreakingly handsome image still haunting her, she was just too tired.

"YOU CAN STOP TALKING ABOUT ME like I'm not here." Dressed in a gray sweatsuit with her feet snug in thick, white socks and her hair crammed into a scrunchie, Stephanie knew she was far from looking her best, but at the moment, her appearance was the least of her worries. With Brady and Olivia sharing the sofa, the twins happily gumming blocks in their playpen, the afternoon should've been idyllic. Far from it. After she'd slept the whole way home, and then crawled directly into bed from there, her best friend and fiancé stared at her as if she'd sprouted alien antennae. "I know I freaked out, and I'm sorry. It won't happen again."

"That's the problem," Brady said, "you obviously don't know when one of these attacks are coming. What if this happened when you're alone with the girls?"

"It won't," she barked, sitting hard on the armchair across from the sofa.

"Honey," Olivia said, her voice softer than Brady's, "we're understandably concerned. Do you have any idea what triggered it? One minute, you were happy and smiling, and the next, out of your mind."

"Thanks," Stephanie said with a heavy dose of sarcasm. "It always makes me feel better knowing my friends are on my side."

"I'm totally on your side," Olivia argued, "but Brady and I are both worried that Lisa may have been right. Maybe you aren't ready for another wedding so soon after losing Michael."

"So soon?" Stephanie shook her head. "It's been

nearly two years. I think that's long enough to sit in my self-imposed depression prison. I'm tired of being sad. I just want things to go back to the way they were meant to be."

"Please don't take this the wrong way," Brady said, "but you do get the fact that I'm not Michael, and never could hope to take his place? I love you, sweetie, but the two of us have to make a fresh start, and if you're still hung up on—"

"Quit," Stephanie pleaded, hands over her ears. "For heaven's sake, I'm over him. Why won't any of you believe me?"

Instantly by her side, Brady knelt, cupping his hands to her knees. "Maybe because you just flipped out in the middle of a bridal store? Sweetie, I hate to say this, but I have to agree with Olivia that maybe marrying so soon isn't the best idea."

"It's a wonderful idea," she snapped. "And you're awful for suggesting what we're doing is wrong."

"That's not what I'm saying. I'm worried about you. We all are."

"Well, stop." Leaning forward, she forced a smile and gave him a kiss. "I'm fine. Great. I had a little setback and it won't happen again."

Chapter Fifteen

"You sure you took your medicine?" Brady asked Steph on board their Seattle-bound flight. He wished he'd been able to fly her out himself, but with his schedule full, there hadn't been time. Steph had seemed anxious through the Little Rock to Dallas leg of their travels.

She nodded.

Holding tight to Steph's cold hand, Brady wasn't sure that with only two weeks until their wedding, flying out for a whirlwind weekend shopping trip for Lola's flower girl dress was a good call, but since Steph had seemed fine since her incident, he'd agreed with her plan. He'd managed to snag first-class seats, which he hoped would help calm her.

With coach-class passengers still streaming by, he said, "We don't have to do this, you know? If you're not feeling it, you can change your mind."

"Why are you making this a big deal?" she asked. "I used to fly all the time. The only reason I had trouble on the way to Miami was because it was the first time I'd flown since Michael died."

"That's all I wanted to know. I love you."

"Me, too." Sleepy from her tranquilizers, she rested her head on his shoulder and promptly fell asleep.

Though Brady was relieved that the flight would be

stress-free, he couldn't help but worry that more was going on with Steph than he knew. Most times they were together, he felt as if he'd known her forever. Then there were days when she seemed quiet and withdrawn. And when he asked what was bothering her, she always said she was tired. But what if it was more? What if she still suffered from depression over Michael's death and her marriage to Brady was nothing more than a bandage for her still-raw wounds?

Another issue nagging him was the fact Steph had never once said she loved him. Oh, she'd shown she cared for him a hundred different ways, but she'd never said the words. A small thing, but important. At least to him.

About twenty minutes from landing, Steph roused. "Did I sleep through the whole flight?"

"Pretty much," he said, kissing her forehead. "You didn't miss anything too exciting."

"I've never flown first class. What was the meal?"

"A little filet mignon, lobster, caviar. The usual."

"And you didn't wake me?" she complained with the cutest pout.

"I'm teasing. Dinner was tasty, but nothing fancy. Some kind of chicken stuff. I'm sure you wouldn't have liked it."

The plane hit a patch of turbulence, causing Steph's face to pale.

"We're fine," he said. "Take deep breaths."

Nodding, she said, "I know. Thank you for putting up with me. I'll be better once we're down."

He stroked her hand. "Why did you want to do this? Clarissa and Lola are perfectly capable of finding a pale pink dress."

"I never said they weren't. I just want to help."

Fidgeting with the end of her seat belt, she added, "Plus, I wanted you to see that I'm over my fear of flying. I know you're worried about my panic attacks, but you need to know I'm better."

"Are you?" He didn't mean to put her on the spot, but he was on the verge of sharing his life with her. If he knew for sure she was better, he'd stop worrying about her. If not, he wanted to make sure she got the best medical care.

"Yes. Of course. You don't believe me?" Her eyes pooled.

"It's not that," he assured her while flight attendants prepared the cabin for landing. "I love you, care about you. You claim to be magically better, but how do you know? Virtually anything could trigger another attack."

Sighing, she turned to gaze out the window. "Do we have to do this now? This trip was supposed to have been fun."

"It will be." He took her hand and brushed her palm with his thumb. "I'm sorry I upset you. That's not at all what I'd intended."

"What did you intend, Brady?"

Rubbing his eyes with his thumb and forefinger, he said, "I don't know. Again, I'm sorry I even brought it up. I thought the whole panic thing was isolated to flying. You're not in the air that often, so taking a pill for relief is a no-brainer. But when you flipped out wedding dress shopping… We're talking a whole new ball game."

"I hardly flipped out." Beneath the cabin, the landing gear clunked into position. Stephanie had a death grip on her seat's armrests.

"An issue of semantics," he said, trying to stay calm.

"Even if you were, let's say, *unsettled,* it's something I'd like you to get checked out."

"You want me to go to a shrink?" Expression mortified, she said under her breath, "My doctor—the one I've been with for over a decade—seems to think I'm fine. There's nothing wrong with me that an occasional dose of medicine won't fix."

Not wanting to rock the boat—or her mood—any further, he acquiesced. "You're right. I'm overreacting, and the fact that you've made it through this flight with no incidents proves you've already made progress."

Snorting, she said, "Thanks for at least admitting that. No matter what you and my friends and my melodramatic sister think, when I'm with you, I don't have a care in the world."

Great. But what about the times when she wasn't with him?

"STEPHANIE," CLARISSA SAID, holding open her front door. To say the house was merely beautiful would be a major understatement. "It's been too long. Lola chats about you and your adorable twins all the time."

"I've heard about you, too," Stephanie said, brushing past her one-time friend with her sleek dark hair and legs that went on for miles. Compared to her, Steph felt like an Oompa Loompa straight out of *Charlie and the Chocolate Factory.*

Lola wasn't yet home from school, and while Brady was outside roughhousing with a lovable sheepdog, Clarissa pulled her aside. "I owe you an apology."

"Oh?" Forgiveness requests seemed to be the day's theme.

"I was mortified when Lola told me she'd told you that I'd called you some, well, unflattering names. It was a bitch move, and I'm sorry. Things with Brady have been tough. Sometimes I find myself just wanting all of this drama to end." With a sad laugh, she added, "Ironic how this time, I was the one to start it."

Taken aback by Clarissa's words, she said, "Um, thanks. I covered for you with Lola as best I could."

"I know." Covering her face with her hands, she admitted, "Lola reported back with your new-and-improved definitions for my words. You acted classy, whereas her own mother did her a disservice. Again, I'm sorry, and I hope we can pick up where we last left off."

"Um…" Surprised by this turn of events, Steph grasped the woman's outstretched hand. "If you'll recall, the last time we were together involved lampshades and way too many margaritas."

They shared a long, cleansing laugh.

"Oh, Steph, I can't believe it's really been that long since we all hung out. Who would've thought dear, funny Michael would be gone and you and Brady would end up together? Crazy, huh?"

Throat aching, all Stephanie could manage was a nod.

"What's going on?" Brady asked, smelling of conifers and the light rain that'd started to fall. After the dog bounded inside, Brady closed the door.

"We're getting reacquainted," Clarissa said. Moving through the open floor plan with gracious ease, she headed for the kitchen. "And for the record, I think you've made an excellent choice for your future bride." Eyes tearing, complexion pale, Clarissa forced cheer. "Now, how about I fix you two up with a nice, hot mug of hot chocolate or tea?"

With a tense quality to his tone that Stephanie hadn't heard before, Brady said, "I'll take a beer."

"Dad!" An hour's worth of excruciatingly awkward small talk later, Lola burst into the house, tossing her book bag to the floor before hurtling herself into Brady's arms. Behind her stood Vince. A taller, thinner, three-years-younger version of Brady who hadn't been out of a suit since third grade. Oh—and Brady forgot to add that Vince also struck him as being perpetually uptight. "I missed you!"

"I missed you, too, pumpkin." Burying his face in her now curly hair, she smelled like peaches. "I'm loving all of these curls. What happened to the straightener?"

"It broke. Mom and I decided that even though Becky likes my hair straight, we like it with my natural wave."

"Great decision," he said, nodding as if they'd decided upon world peace.

"And, Stephanie!" Flinging herself a short distance sideways on the sofa, the little girl landed on his fiancée's lap. "I can't wait to find a dress!"

Brady loved the way his daughter once again spoke in exclamations. It returned him to the joy of his childhood. The way he'd had no worries other than what to do with his day. Fishing. Beachcombing. Playing pirate with Vince and their friends. Endless possibilities. Endless fun. He wanted the same for his daughter. Judging by her smiling reunion with Stephanie, his choice of stepmoms was spot-on. And if Lola's devotion to her was any indication, his worries about Stephanie being emotionally *off* were unfounded.

From now on, he wouldn't look for trouble where there

was none. Like his jubilant little girl, with Stephanie by his side, he would laugh and live and love.

Thirty minutes later, while Lola showed Steph her tree house, Brady found his way back inside to catch Clarissa and Vince kissing. A few months earlier, the sight would've sent him over the edge. Now, he was happy that Clarissa was in a good place. It made it all the easier for him to move on to his own slice of happiness.

Clearing his throat, he said, "Sorry to interrupt, but we need to talk."

"Sure, bro." Vince had loosened his tie and unfastened the top couple of buttons of his starched white shirt. "What's up?"

As if tensing for an ambush, Clarissa tightened her grip on Vince's waist.

"First off, relax." He tried smiling, and found it wasn't the impossibility it used to be whenever he was around these two. "I don't want to fight anymore, but apologize."

Their mutual relieved sigh was audible.

"Oh, come on," he said with a half smile, "have things between us really been that bad?"

Both nodding, their smiles were tentative.

Ramming his hands in his jean pockets, Brady looked away. Ashamed that as the older of the two, he'd let things between him and his brother deteriorate to this level.

"Brady," Vince finally said, "you've gotta know neither of us planned for this—*us*—to happen."

"Yeah. I know. I screwed up and you were there to pick up the pieces."

"It was hardly that simple," Clarissa said. "You and I, Brady, we just crumpled. Like the foundation of our marriage had been torn out from under us. In a hundred years, I don't think we could pinpoint every little thing that went wrong. And at this point, why would we want to?"

Nodding, a muscle working in his jaw, Brady figured that just about summed it up. Somewhere in between his reunion with Steph, he'd lost the will to fight. His animosity for two of his former best friends was gone. In its place grew cautious optimism that in the future, for Lola's sake, and even their own, they might once again be friends.

As WOULD ANY TRUE PRINCESS, on Saturday, with Stephanie by her side, Lola proudly picked her own flower girl dress. It was shell-pink with a skirt sprinkled in crystals and darker pink silk roses. Admiring herself in the dressing room mirror, she said, "Becky's gonna be *soooo* jealous."

Laughing, Stephanie said, "I've got to meet this girl before your dad and I head back to Arkansas."

"Okay," she said, twirling in a circle with her arms stretched wide. "I'll ask Mom if she can sleep over."

"That sounds fun." Gathering the dresses Lola hadn't chosen from a burgundy velvet bench, Steph said, "When they get older, you'll have to teach the twins how to have the perfect sleepover party."

"Okay." Shimmying free of her dress, she asked, "Where are you and my dad going on your honeymoon?"

"You know, we've been so busy planning for the ceremony that I haven't even thought about it."

"Becky says that's when grown-ups go someplace fun without their kids so that they can kiss and stuff." She tugged on purple jeans and a sparkly white unicorn sweater. "Sounds gross to me, but the vacation part would be okay."

Biting back a laugh, Steph strove to match the girl's solemn expression. "I agree," she said with a stern nod. "I'll have to tell your father that wherever we go, I want more fun and less kissing. Blech."

Lola held up her hand for a high five.

Stephanie met it, but only halfway. "Let me try that again," she said, this time meeting the girl's palm square-on.

"Why are you shaking?"

"I don't know," she confessed, telling the truth. "Probably wedding nerves."

In all seriousness, Lola said, "Becky talks a lot about those. She said her mom's favorite medicine for that is vodka."

"How did the shopping go?" Brady asked when Stephanie returned to her hotel room. He'd offered to put her up at his apartment, but out of respect for Lola, she'd politely declined.

"Exhausting, but fun," she said, collapsing onto one of two cream-colored armchairs in front of floor-to-ceiling windows. The view of Mount Ranier was impressive, but not nearly as awe-inspiring as his bride.

"I'm glad you're back." Putting the Snickers wrapper he'd been using for a bookmark in his adventure novel, he pushed himself up from the bed. He knelt in front of her and rested his head in her lap. Her jeans were still cold from the outside, and smelled woodsy. He loved that about the Northwest. How everything carried with it the reminder that nature was bigger than any of them.

Combing his hair with her fingers, she said, "I'm even more glad to be back. Lola's quite a handful."

Chuckling, he glanced up at her. "What trouble did her mouth get her into this time?"

"She not only wanted to know where we were going for our honeymoon, but if we were going to kiss."

"What did you tell her?" Grasping her hands, he blew warm breath on the tips of her chilled fingers.

"Essentially that we would try not to—kiss."

"Oh, yeah?" Pushing up the sleeves of her thin red sweater, he said, "So this wouldn't qualify?" He pressed his lips to her wrists, blazing an erotic trail all the way to her inner elbow.

When she squirmed and giggled, he knew he'd found the right spot.

"Or this?" Raising her sweater's hem, he forged a leisurely exploration of her abdomen.

"Stop…" She halfheartedly protested even while raising her hips into his kiss. Shaking her head, she made cute panting noises when he unbuttoned her jeans and nipped at her white lace panties. "Never mind… Keep going…"

"You don't have to ask me twice." Pushing aside all clothing blocking his way, he gently parted her legs, kissing her inner thighs and then more. Her hands in his hair, she pulled hard, moaning and bucking after each breathy exhale.

Once she'd cried out in pleasure, he made hasty work of removing his clothes.

Scooping her weak-limbed into his arms, he set her on the bed, proceeding with the all-important business of practicing for their first official night as man and wife.

"AND YOU WERE FINE ON all four legs of your trip to Seattle?" Dr. Naomi Hembro asked the Wednesday before the wedding. Stephanie had loads of much more important matters to attend to, but without telling Brady or her nosy sister and friends, she'd made the appointment more as a reassurance to herself that she was all right than for any of them.

"Absolutely. I didn't have a lick of trouble." Remembering their last night in their posh hotel brought on a rush of heat. Luckily a quick glance at her current sterile surroundings brought her overheated imagination back to the normal zone.

"Did you take tranquilizers at least thirty minutes before flying?"

Stephanie nodded while her friend made notes on her chart.

"Describe what happened in the bridal shop. Were you feeling claustrophobic or overheated?"

"No. Best as I can remember, it was sleeting that day, so if anything, I was probably cold." What she didn't tell her doctor was that she remembered exactly what'd triggered her irrational fear. Michael. A rush of tangible memories that haunted her to this day.

And then there were the hand tremors, striking out of nowhere with such severity she could hardly sign her name. But that didn't have anything to do with Brady or the wedding, right?

"Sounds to me as if this is just a case of situational anxiety. Understandably, fear of flying is a trigger to many people. The bridal shop incident, though, still puzzles me." Jotting more notes, and then writing a name on one of her prescription pad sheets, the woman said, "I want you to speak with a therapist. She's a longtime friend of mine who specializes in grief management."

"But I'm fine with what happened to Michael," Steph protested, not at all pleased that her doctor and future husband were on the same page in regard to her mental health.

"Your loss would be hard for anyone to deal with. Throw in running your own business and single-handedly raising infant twins, and anyone would be under extreme pressure."

"I love my life," Stephanie said, fishing through her purse for a stick of cinnamon gum. Her hands shook so badly, she was glad for the cover. "I'm getting married in less than a week and feel better than I ever have."

Sitting on a low stool, the doctor said, "Please don't take this the wrong way, but if everything in your life is so wonderful, why are you here?"

Chapter Sixteen

The doctor's question bugged Stephanie all the way back to the shop. If her issues with Michael's death had been resolved, going to her family physician wouldn't have been necessary. So much in her daily life had changed for the better. Why was she then finding it impossible to forget her former life? Why was she consumed with thoughts that if she did marry Brady, she'd only end up losing him, too? And she wasn't just caught up in the whole pilot thing. The odds of him also dying in a crash were practically nil. But there were other ways to lose a husband.

Disease.

Another woman.

Being a big enough nut job that he'd rather be single than stay with you....

With Valentine's Day that weekend, she'd hired three local women for temporary help at the pastry shop. Ordinarily, she and her usual staff would've handled the added holiday load, but it'd been a matter of great pride to her to make her own wedding cake.

She'd already been working on the five-tiered creation for a day, and due to the complex lace icing pattern, she fully expected it to take until Friday to finish.

"Where have you been?" Helen asked, wiping her

hands on a white apron. "We've got orders backed up, and the register is completely out of change."

"I'll run down to the bank," Stephanie said, neatly sidestepping the issue of where she'd spent the past hour. "Need anything else?"

"You look feverish." Her friend held the backs of her fingers to Steph's forehead. "But you don't feel hot. A good thing being so perilously close to your big day."

"Be right back," Stephanie said, taking the large bills from the register and slipping them into a green zippered bank bag.

"Steph, your hands are shaking like a leaf."

"It's wicked cold outside. Brrr." She rubbed her hands up and down her arms to emphasize the degree of her chill, and to hide her little white lie about what was truly going on.

She hated dodging Helen, but it was as necessary as getting to the florist to confirm her wedding order.

At the bank, Stephanie ran into two high school friends who asked too many questions about Brady. She was thrilled to be marrying him, but the closer the ceremony came, the more superstitious she grew. As though if she talked about it too much, it might never happen.

"So there we were," Clarissa said to everyone assembled at the rehearsal dinner that Olivia and Tag had volunteered to host at their house, "walking for hours up the glacier at Lake Louise, when all of the sudden this momma grizzly and her two cubs stepped out of the woods." Guzzling the last of her white wine, she signaled to a hired waiter. "Well, you should've seen Vince. He squealed like a third-grade girl."

"Did not," he protested, "in fact, if I remember

correctly, you were the one who said you nearly peed your pants."

"Yes, but I am a girl," she pointed out, after which Brady's parents, Gloria and Charles, practically fell out of their chairs laughing.

Stephanie's mom, Phyllis, too.

She'd flown in from Tucson for the occasion. She wasn't at all what Brady had expected. Much taller than Steph and her twin, the woman had brown eyes and short-cropped brown hair. From her stares, he got the impression Phyllis had been talking a little too much with Lisa, who never failed to remind her sister that the wedding had come about too fast.

Speaking of Steph's evil twin, she spent the bulk of the night alternately scowling and/or cozying up to a never-empty glass of merlot.

Excusing himself, Brady left the dining room to hide out for a few minutes in one of the three living areas. The house was more like a hotel with so many rooms he'd lost count. But their host and hostess were cool. Unaffected by their apparent wealth.

Standing before a wall of windows overlooking the Arkansas River, he tried recalling how he'd gotten to this point. To a night where he was on the verge of marrying one woman, while his first wife was partying with his brother and their folks. It was nuts.

"Brady?" the only voice of sanity in his life said. "You okay? When you didn't come back I got worried about you. Thought you might've gotten lost."

"I did," he said with a sigh, "but since you've found me, I'm thinking I'm going to be okay."

Easing her arms around him, she rested her cheek against his chest. "We're both going to be great," she assured. "And just think, by tomorrow at this time, I'm going to be Mrs. Brady McGuire."

Kissing her slowly and sweetly, he said, "I like the sound of that."

"I've got something to tell you," she stood on her tiptoes to whisper into his right ear. "In case I failed to mention it back in Seattle, you're *waaaay* cuter than your brother."

Laughing, he asked, "How is it you always know the right thing to say?"

"It's a gift," she said, the light from the river reflecting in her eyes. "And it's about to be yours for the low, low price of a wedding ring."

"And flowers," he tagged on with a smile. "And don't forget the dress and caterer bill."

"You just had to bring all of that up, didn't you?" Back on her tiptoes, she kissed him right back.

"I'm pretty sure one of my marital duties is to nag about how much money you spend."

Adopting her best British accent, she said, "Then I shall try to be careful with your vast financial holdings."

"That would be most appreciated, fair wench."

A smile tickling her lips, she said, "I'm so excited about tomorrow. You're going to make a great husband."

"Ditto." He kissed her forehead. "I love you."

Snuggling against him, she said, "Me, too."

"KNOCK, KNOCK."

Upon hearing her sister at the nursery door at well past midnight, Stephanie clutched her chest. In a loud whisper, she demanded, "What are you doing here?"

Joining her alongside Melanie's crib, Lisa said, "I

used my key. I know it's late, but we need to talk. You're my best friend, and I can't take this tension between us."

That made two of them. But Lisa had made it abundantly clear she was dead set against Stephanie's upcoming marriage. Without a major apology, she wasn't about to kiss and make up. It was only because their mother had begged that Lisa had even been invited back into the wedding party.

"Steph, I'm sorry if I've come across as the grim reaper of weddings, but I know you better than anyone. You're not ready for taking this huge of a step. I like Brady. A lot. He's amazing with you and the girls, but he's not Michael. You might say you're ready to move on, but I saw your hands tremble tonight at the rehearsal dinner whenever the topic was broached about you and Brady being together forever. You're terrified inside of not only maybe losing him, but of one day giving him up when you realize he doesn't measure up to Michael."

Turning her back on her sister, Stephanie stormed out of the room. With the nursery door closed, and Lisa hot on her heels, she said, "Thought you came here to apologize. Not deliver more insults."

Dropping to the sofa, Stephanie grabbed a white throw pillow to hug. "Do you have any idea how bad it hurts for my other half to not be able to see how amazing Brady and I are together?"

"Oh, sweetie," Lisa said, perching beside her, taking her hand, "that's not at all what I mean. I want you to start fresh. I want you to be happy. But I want you to do it in a healthy way. This thing with Brady happened too fast. How many times did you tell me the two of you were just friends? And then, poof! All of a sudden you're wearing a huge ring and asking me to babysit his daughter. Can't you see that the root of your panic is that your heart hasn't caught up with your head?"

"W-why are you doing this?" Stephanie asked, her voice small and defeated. "Why can't you just shut up and let me be happy?" She turned her back to her twin. "You've never lost a husband. You've never raised two babies on your own. You've never run your own business and—"

"I know. Stop reminding me of all the ways I'm not as good as you long enough to hear what I'm truly saying." Taking her hands and holding them tight, Lisa said, "I love you. Plain as that. If marrying Brady is the fulfillment of your every dream, then from here on, I vow to shut up and fully support you. My twin radar is off, and again, I'm so sorry for doubting you."

"Thank you." Stephanie angled to better face her sister. "You know how much I love you, which is why having you disapprove of my wedding has hurt so bad. Lisa, please, stop making me hurt. I've been through enough and now I just want to smile."

"Th-that's all I want for you." With Lisa now crying, too, they hugged it out.

Finally earning Lisa's seal of approval had been the crowning touch needed for Stephanie's happy day.

"I'm sooooo ready to get married!" Extra hyper during the thirty minutes before the wedding, Lola spun and hopped in her pretty pink dress. Her impromptu dance didn't make the historic chapel's cramped bridal suite feel any larger.

"Me, too," Stephanie said, only for the not-so-admirable reason that she just wanted to get it over with. She hadn't been prepared for the onslaught of Brady's relatives. Clarissa and Vince, around whom he was understandably on edge. Then there were his parents, a parade of aunts and uncles. Cousins who had a never ending stream of Arkansas hillbilly jokes.

"You okay?" Olivia asked. She looked beautiful in her red velvet strapless gown. As did Gabby and Lisa. For the twins, she'd found an antique white-wicker baby carriage that she'd lined with white satin. Both girls wore frothy pink dresses and had tiny bows in their curly hair.

Nodding, Stephanie said, "Last night was fun, but took a lot out of me. Who knew Brady's family was large enough to populate a small country. Thanks again for hosting."

"It was my pleasure—Tag's, too. You know how he likes throwing parties."

"Yeah." At the mention of the party, Stephanie's memory went back in time to her first wedding reception. She and Michael had been so young, as had most of their guests. High school and culinary school friends who knew how to have a good time. Once the garden ceremony had finished, Michael's best man had fired up the grill, and out came a keg for the guys and dangerously liquored-up punch for the girls. Lisa's then-boyfriend had driven a truck that he'd retrofitted with a DJ station in the bed. A ghost of a smile playing about her lips, she couldn't remember ever having danced harder, or having more fun.

"What're you thinking about?" Olivia asked.

Jolted from her thoughts, Stephanie met her reflection in the antique vanity table's mirror. Far from bridal, she looked wide-eyed and terrified. Forcing a smile, she said, "I'm hoping I'll be a great wife."

"Of course, you will," her co-matron of honor assured. "Brady loves you so much, and anyone can see you love him."

Stephanie's eyes teared and her pulse raced. Her emotions felt dangerously close to being out of control. Breathing deeply, by sheer will, she held it together.

"You all right?" her mother asked. It'd been so long since she'd seen her and despite being in her thirties, Stephanie very much needed a hug from her mom.

Holding out her arms, trying not to cry, she whispered, "I love you. Thank you so much for being here."

"Where else would I be? I'm so proud of you. Lots of my friends in Tucson who lose their husbands fold up shop and wait to die. Sure, they're older than you—" she fussed over a few of Steph's runaway curls "—but age doesn't make your decision to put the past in the past any easier."

Sniffling, Stephanie nodded.

"Stop all of this frowning," her mom commanded. "You're a bride. You're required to be luminous and so gorgeous that all of the bridesmaids want to run away and hide."

Laughing, crying, Stephanie agreed.

"DAMN, I'M GOOD-LOOKIN'," Brady boasted of himself a few minutes before heading out to the stone church's sanctuary.

"And not a bit conceited," his best man, Pete, said with a few pats to his back.

Also standing up for him were Neil Myers, a longtime friend from flight school, and Vince. Since Brady had owned up to the role he'd played in his marriage's collapse, the two had slowly been working their way back to being true brothers. Since Vince had stood up for him at his first wedding, Brady felt it fitting that his brother also stand up for him now, at the start of the rest of his life with Steph.

From outside the office where the guys had been told to assemble came a knock.

Neil opened the door to find the elderly pastor who would be performing the ceremony. "Where's my groom? Is he ready?"

"As I'll ever be," Brady quipped. All teasing aside, he was psyched. It might've come about in whirlwind style, but his marriage to Steph was going to be great. They'd have more kids, and maybe snag a bigger house closer to a hub airport so he wouldn't have such a long commute.

"That's what I like to hear," the man said. When he smiled, his bushy eyebrows nearly connected with his thick head of white hair.

Standing at the altar, Brady was blown away by the decorating job Steph and her friends had done on the sanctuary. With stone walls and plenty of stained-glass windows, the place was already beautiful, but with the ceremony set to begin at six, and hundreds of candles illuminating the otherwise dark space, the old church was luminescent.

Adding to the romance theme were the red roses he'd requested. Far too many to count paired with ivy and tons of other pale and hot-pink blooms that were too fancy for him to know the names. Festoons of fragrant blossoms lined the pews and the altar had become a candlelit wonderland.

Making a mental note to thank Steph for doing an outstanding job of making their wedding memorable, he looked out at the sea of family and friends. Many of them knew of his rocky past. There weren't enough words to describe how happy he was to put all of that behind him.

The string octet finished their current piece, and then began a more familiar classical tune.

There was a commotion in the chapel's vestibule, and then out popped Lola down the aisle. She smiled and twirled and to the delight of everyone assembled, tossed an assortment of rose petals that landed on just about all surfaces but the floor.

His aunt Martha looked a little miffed by the half a rosebush that'd landed on her helmet hair.

When his daughter reached him, he knelt for a hug, whispering in her ear, "Great job."

"Thanks, Dad!" Though still fidgety and all smiles, she did her best to stay put in her assigned spot.

Next down the aisle were Steph's twin and then Gabby. Upon first hearing about Stephanie's identical sister, he'd worried he wouldn't be able to tell them apart, but to him they looked nothing alike. Steph had an innate softness Lisa lacked.

Olivia finished up the procession, looking regal in her long red gown.

The wedding march began and all assembled rose to face the bride.

At his first sight of his future wife being escorted by Tag, Brady's heart swelled. Lord, she was gorgeous. Through eyes welling with emotions ranging from gratitude to the deepest of loves, he drank in her long, loose hair. Ringlets cascading her shoulders in a cloud. With her every step, the stones of her tiara and a myriad of crystals sewn into her gown reflected the candlelight.

The only thing missing was her smile.

The closer she came, the more he noted the tremble in her bouquet. The wild-eyed panic in her eyes. It was the same look she'd worn when he'd first seen her again all those months ago on the plane.

For all of her protests that she was emotionally fine, he recognized all too well the signs that she was hanging on by a very thin thread.

When she reached him, he leaned down to kiss her cheek, whispering, "Relax, sweetheart. Everything's going to be fine. I'm here with you. Nothing's ever going to hurt you again."

She nodded, but didn't meet his eyes.

"I love you," he said, his fingers beneath her chin.

Again, she shattered him with only a nod.

They were on the verge of spending the rest of their lives together. Why wouldn't she look at him? Let him in?

The pastor cleared his throat. "Who gives this woman to be wed?"

"I do," Tag said, while Olivia took Steph's trembling bouquet.

With her hands in his, Brady held them as firm as he dared, trying to convey to her, without making a scene, that everything was going to be okay.

But was it?

The further into their vows the pastor went, the more pale Steph grew. Her breaths came shallow and her eyes took on an erratic dart.

Following the pastor's directions, he said, "I, Brady, do hereby take you, Stephanie, to be my lawfully wedded wife."

She started to cry.

"To have and to hold…"

Her light tremble grew to the point that her entire body now shook.

"To love and to cherish…"

She gasped for breath.

"In sickness or in health…"

Ripping her hands from his, she clawed at the bodice of her gown.

"For as long as we both shall—"

"I'm sorry," she said with an anguished cry. "I can't do this. I—I have to get out of here. The walls are closing in." Abandoning him at the altar, she ran down the aisle.

Her tiara clattered to the floor.

Chasing her, Brady accidentally kicked the crown of silver and crystal on his way out the door.

Bursting through the chapel's double doors, he found her hunched over in the attached graveyard, shivering in the brutal cold. A wind had whipped up, swirling leaves and creaking branches.

"What's wrong with you?" he cried. "This was what you wanted. *You* asked to marry me."

She dropped to her knees and sobbed. "I—I know. But I'm afraid. I already l-lost Michael and you're a pilot and what if I'm not really over him and I don't know what I was thinking because I clearly can't marry you."

"Bullshit," he raged. "This has nothing to do with us. Michael flew in a war zone. I fly business travelers and tourists. There's a huge difference. Statistically, you're much safer—"

"I don't care!" she screamed. "All right, so this has nothing to do with you flying, and everything to do with my shattered heart. I won't marry you. I'll never marry you. I can't go through losing another man I love."

"You're not being rational. Where's your medication?" he asked, glancing toward the chapel, at the throng of gawking guests standing at the doors. "Did you bring it?"

"I don't want a pill, Brady." Wind whipped her hair in her face. It was a dark night, but even from the glow emanating through the chapel windows, he saw black streaking from her eyes. "I don't want you. I can't do this. Keep living a lie."

Her words sliced him to his core.

Dropping to his knees, sitting back on his haunches, he put his hand to his forehead, struggling for a logical way out. Where was the funny and warm and talented woman he'd fallen in love with? Why couldn't he bring her back?

"I love you," he said quietly, not knowing or caring if she heard him above the wind. "I love you and you're throwing me away. I told you to get help. You were too stubborn to admit anything was wrong. Well, you know what?" he asked through gritted teeth. "I'm done. I've already been decimated by one woman I loved, and I'll be damned if it ever happens again."

Rising to his feet, he ignored Stephanie's ever-increasing wails.

"Not only have you hurt me," he cruelly said, "but you've also hurt my daughter. And it'll be a cold day in hell before I speak to you again." Turning his back on her, he mounted the chapel steps, picked up his crying and confused little girl, and wound through the crowded lot to find his rented car.

Chapter Seventeen

"Dad?" Lola asked from the lanai of the private Maui beach house he'd planned to surprise Stephanie with for their honeymoon.

"Yes?" He'd stretched out in the hammock, trying to sleep, but that, just like every other escape he strove for, wouldn't seem to come. His ex-bride had made him numb.

"I know I asked why Stephanie left us before, but I still don't get it." She made her Barbie do the splits on the glass-topped table. "Steph told me she loved me. But if she loved me, why did she want to hurt me like that?"

Aching for not only himself, but his daughter, he fought stinging eyes. He'd vowed to not cry one more tear for that woman, and unlike her, he kept his promises.

Eyes closed, he surrendered himself to the balmy breeze stroking his bare arms, legs and chest. He focused on the surf's roar and the salt-flavored air. The tropical paradise would be his place to heal. When the week was up, he'd emerge a better, stronger man for having weathered Stephanie's storm.

"Dad?" With a start, he looked up to find Lola standing over him. "You didn't answer." Climbing into the hammock, she snuggled alongside him, clinging to him like she hadn't since she'd been very young.

"Baby, I wish I had an answer for you. Something that would magically make you feel better, but the truth is, I don't think even Stephanie knows why she left."

"Are the twins going to be okay? I really miss them."

"They'll be fine." He hoped. Steph had a huge support system, if only she'd open herself to letting them in.

"I'm mad at Stephanie, but I still love her. Think we'll see her again?"

Kissing her forehead, he said, "I don't know, baby. I don't know."

IT'D BEEN A WEEK SINCE the wedding.

A week during which Stephanie had returned all of the lovely gifts, each accompanied by a handwritten apology note.

Since running out on her wedding, she hadn't experienced a shred of the panic that'd held her in its grip. Point of fact, aside from embarrassment and loneliness and the pain of hurting so many people she loved, physically she'd never felt better.

Following her doctor's advice, she'd called the therapist Naomi had recommended. After two emergency sessions, she was now scheduled to visit every Wednesday afternoon.

With the twins down for a nap, she found herself at loose ends. She'd already tidied, done laundry and dusted her few knickknacks. Maybe she'd been hasty in hiring two responsible teens to run the shop on Saturdays?

No. Her therapist said it was good for her to spend time with her girls, reminding herself of what was positive in her life, rather than focusing on the bad.

In her bedroom, she changed the sheets on her bed. She'd bought the cheery floral print in anticipation of Brady sharing them. He'd ribbed her about the master bedroom being too girly, but all-in-all, he'd been a good sport.

She was changing pillowcases when she fumbled and dropped one to the floor. Kneeling next to the bed, a corner of sky-blue caught her eye. It was the special Christmas gift she'd found for Brady. The one she'd bid way too much for in an online auction, but hadn't been able to resist because she'd known how much Brady would love it.

Painstakingly unwrapping the box, she recalled how intense the auction process had been. How she'd wanted to wait to give it to him when they'd found a private moment alone. But then he'd kissed her and things had moved on from there. She was asking him to marry her and he'd agreed and their lives had been a whirlwind from there.

Lifting the box's lid, she fished through layers of tissue to pull out the leather-bound, author-signed copy of *20 Hrs., 40 Min.: Our Flight in the Friendship,* written by Brady's idol, Amelia Earhart.

Clutching the rare treasure to her chest, thinking of what a gem the gift's recipient had been, she cried.

"IT'S INTERESTING TO ME," Stephanie's therapist said during her next appointment, "that the first time you've cried since the wedding, was over a present Brady never received. Do you see the correlation? How you've cried over the loss of your first husband, but now your subconscious has added Brady to your list of loved ones to be mourned?"

Shifting her position on the sofa in the office that had

been decorated to resemble a living room, Stephanie said, "I get it, but what am I supposed to do about it? Since walking out on Brady, all I do is miss him, but I know that if he were to somehow be stupid enough to take me back, I'd just flip out again. I mean, I thought what I was afraid of was losing him, but all along, I think I've been scared of losing myself. The woman I was when Michael and I were together." Fingers pressed to her temples, she admitted, "Why can't I get it through my head that I'll never be that woman again? And that it's okay for me to reinvent myself with Brady?"

"During the coming week," the willowy brunette said, adjusting her black-framed glasses, "I want you to focus on not being so hard on yourself. Take one of your earlier statements for instance. If Brady would be *stupid* enough to want to give you a second chance. From everything I've gathered, you are a kind, loving woman and mother who has understandably lost her way. Why are you so quick to forgive others, but not Stephanie?"

Eyes stinging, she shook her head.

"Do you think you're not worthy of love?"

"No. Just now I think I've grasped the concept that until I'm over Michael, I'm not capable of giving love. And maybe I'm even feeling guilty for having the second chance Michael never had."

With an ironic chuckle, the therapist said, "Very intuitive revelation. Hate to be the bearer of bad news, but there are times in all of our lives when the best solution is falling back to regroup. Stephanie, in realizing that, you've taken a major first step in healing." Her smile was congratulatory. "What you need to do now is release the guilt and give yourself permission to live. Think you can do that?"

No, Stephanie wasn't at all sure. Still, she owed it not only to herself and her girls, but to Brady and Lola to try.

THAT NIGHT, STEPHANIE FED and bathed the twins, and then tucked them in for the night. When she was sure both were sleeping soundly, she popped the cork of the nice bottle of red she'd picked up on her way home, and without bothering with a glass, took a deep swig.

She had a big evening ahead of her.

Her therapy session had been illuminating. Most of all for the fact that she had subconsciously felt guilty for once again having fun. Well, no more.

Sitting on the edge of the bed, wine bottle on the nightstand, she reached for one of her favorite photos of Michael. The one of the two of them at his family picnic. Skimming the pad of her thumb over his smiling image, she asked, "What am I going to do, Michael?"

It hurt that his family never called. She got the fact that his mom was still grieving, but didn't she realize that a part of him lived on right here in Valley View? Wasn't she the least bit curious about the miracle Michael had left behind?

"We sure made pretty babies," she said, drinking more wine. *Made,* being the relevant term. What they shared had been the stuff dreams are made of, but what she and Brady shared was every bit as special. In holding so tight to her past, she'd essentially thrown away her future. "Thank you for my girls," she whispered. "But now, for me, for them, I've got to let you go."

It took more wine, but she found the emotional strength to gather not only Michael's photos, but his few clothes. A TransGlobal sweatshirt she wore on especially cold and lonely nights. Ticket stubs from their first fancy night out when they'd seen *The Phantom of the Opera*.

Faster and faster she worked, stunned to discover how empty her bedroom looked with Michael well and truly gone. Stephanie felt at peace knowing his stuff might be safely tucked into a box for Michaela and Melanie to one day explore, but the most important part of him—his love—she would always safely hold inside.

How many times had he told her that should anything ever happen to him, his wish for her was to go on? He didn't want her engaging in random hook-ups but in the real deal—just like what they'd shared. In Brady she'd found that. Different. Yet at the core—the love—so very much the same.

After taking the snapshot of Michael removing her wedding garter from its silver frame, she replaced it with one of him playing soccer with a bunch of Iraqi orphans. The photo told of his commitment to making the world a better place. One child at a time. Even if the only way he knew to help was by making them smile.

Rising, she crept into the nursery, then set the photo on a shelf next to the changing table. It was important to her that the girls know their father. But it was just as important that they grew to love their new daddy.

That is, if Brady agreed to let her back into his life.

Over the coming days, she had some big decisions. From her perspective, though, the toughest—jumping back into life—had just been made.

BRIGHT AND EARLY THE NEXT morning, confident in her new directions, Stephanie asked Olivia to watch the girls for a few days, and then sat down for a heart-to-heart with Helen. Leaving the pastry shop with a handshake and promise, she made a brief stop at Lisa's office and then started off on what would surely be the biggest adventure she'd ever had. As expected, her twin had been worried, but this time, once Stephanie explained the breakthrough she'd had at the counselor and then later at home, Lisa had gifted her with a hug and teary well wishes.

In Seattle, a steady downpour made it tough going in finding Brady's apartment. Once she did, as luck would have it, he wasn't home. Sure, she could've called, but considering how gravely she'd botched things up between them, if she were to have any chance at reconciling, she wanted to have that meeting in person.

She also needed to make things right with Lola, starting by delivering a major apology. Since it was only three in the afternoon and Lola didn't get out of school until three-thirty, Stephanie struck out for Clarissa and Vince's, praying they'd at least let her in.

Parked in the drive in front of their home, Stephanie prayed for calm and surprisingly got it. Since pinpointing her panic hot buttons, her frayed nerves seemed to have exponentially improved. Today was the last big hurdle.

Forcing a deep breath, she jumped from the car and made a mad dash through the rain. On the covered porch, she tried making herself presentable, but gave up. Hopefully, Lola or Brady wouldn't make their decision on whether or not to take her back based upon her dripping hair!

"What are you doing here?" Clarissa only halfway opened the door. "Haven't you already caused enough trouble?"

"Yes, but…" Stephanie willed her pulse to slow. She made this mess. It was her obligation to clean it up. "Look, I don't blame you for being angry on Lola's behalf. What I did was unforgivable, but I'm better now—or, at least getting there—and part of the process is making amends with the people I love."

Expression dubious, Clarissa stepped aside, gesturing for Stephanie to enter the house. Without saying a word, Clarissa left her standing on the stone-floored entry. A minute later, she returned with a plush navy towel. "Dry yourself off. You're a mess."

"Thanks."

Once Stephanie was no longer dripping, Clarissa put on a fresh pot of coffee.

Seated at the kitchen table, Clarissa asked, "Why today? What's happened to make you suddenly worthy of a second chance?"

As succinctly as she could, Stephanie explained her therapy and issues with grief, and how badly she needed Lola and Brady to know her wedding-day meltdown had nothing to do with them and everything to do with her own insecurities.

Once Stephanie had worked herself into a fresh round of tears, Clarissa rounded the table to crush her in a hug. "I'm so glad you came. Since the wedding, Lola's been in a serious funk. While I can't speak for Brady, our little girl will be happy you're here."

"I hope so," Stephanie said, drying her eyes with a tissue Clarissa had given her.

"As for Brady, he's on a two-day layover in Chicago. Feel like waiting?"

Stephanie shook her head.

"Didn't think so."

Clarissa gave her the name and number of Brady's Chicago hotel.

"Mom!" Lola hollered after slamming the door. "I'm home!"

Stomach a mess, Stephanie rose, whispering to Clarissa, "Do I look okay?"

"Beautiful." Heading for the living room, she signaled for Stephanie to follow. To Lola she said, "Look who came for a visit."

Lola's smile faded. "You hurt my dad and I hate you!" The girl chased off to her room.

Stephanie started to follow, but Clarissa stopped her. "Give her space. I'll talk to her." Halfway up the stairs, Clarissa turned to say, "For what it's worth. I'm on your side. Nothing would make me happier than to see things between you and Brady work out."

THIRTY LONG MINUTES LATER, Stephanie still paced the kitchen, pausing every so often for a fortifying sip of coffee. What was she doing here? Obviously, she'd overestimated her importance in Lola's life. And if that was the case, what would her reception with Brady be? Did he also feel this strongly about never seeing her again?

She'd just gathered her coat and purse to quietly leave when Lola asked from the top of the stairs, "Are you leaving?"

"If that's what you want me to do…" Staring up at Brady's precious little girl, Stephanie's limbs felt frozen.

"No. Please stay." Racing down the stairs, Lola nearly toppled her with the force of her hug. "I'm sorry. Mom told me what happened to you and I didn't know your heart was sick. I thought you just stopped loving me and Dad."

"Never," Stephanie said. *More like I stopped loving myself.* "No matter what, pumpkin, I will always love you."

Clarissa was next racing down the stairs, only she was grabbing car keys. "Okay, gang, love, love, hug, hug, let's go." She held open the door.

"What's wrong with you, Mom?" Lola cocked her head with her hands on her hips. "Me and Steph are having a conversation."

"That's wonderful, baby, but finish in the car. I just booked her on a 5:40 p.m. flight to Chicago and in order to make it, we're going to have to hustle."

"What about my rental?"

Rolling her eyes, Clarissa held out her hand. "Give me the keys, and Vince and I will return it in the morning. Right now, let's get you on the plane."

Chapter Eighteen

For Stephanie, compared to the nightmare of possibly never having Brady in her life, flying had become no big deal—especially since Clarissa had snagged her a first-class upgrade. She was still a nervous wreck, but more out of anticipation than fear.

Upon landing at O'Hare International well past midnight, she had no problem finding a taxi to take her to the man she wanted to spend the rest of her life with. Trouble was, did he feel the same about her?

In the Marriott's lobby, for security reasons, the check-in clerk refused to give Stephanie Brady's room number. She did, however, agree to let her talk to him on the phone.

"Brady," she said, "It's Stephanie, and before you hang up, please give me your room number. I have to see you."

"Where are you?" he asked.

"Here. In Chicago. We need to talk."

"Do you realize what time it is?" His groggy, less-than-thrilled tone told her she'd made a mistake in coming.

Her broken heart told her to stay the course.

"Please, Brady," she urged, not above begging. "Please tell me where you are."

Sighing, he said, "Nine-ten."

IN THE MINUTES IT TOOK Steph to grab an elevator and find his room, Brady was pretty sure he was going to puke. How many times had he rehearsed what he'd say in the unlikely event of this very meeting? Yet now, his mind was blank.

Like a surgeon, he'd tried so hard to cut her from his life. He tried not thinking about her. He'd even gone so far as to try throwing away all reminders of her. Key word in all of the above being *try*. Only to ultimately fail.

Lord help him, but he still loved her.

When she knocked, he rested his forehead against the door. Part of him wanted to see her more than anything in the world. Another part knew she'd only bring more pain.

"Brady?" she said with another knock. "Let me in."

He did, stepping aside for her to pass.

With the curtains drawn, the generic space felt tight.

Perched on the foot of the king-size bed, she set her purse on the floor.

"What?" he asked, arms folded. After closing the door, he still stood there. His feet refused to move.

"Could you please sit down?" she asked, patting the space beside her.

"I can't." To sit alongside her would only make her eventual leaving that much harder to bear.

Her lower lip quivered.

He wanted to go to her, but the gnawing ache in his chest where his heart used to be wouldn't let him. She hadn't just hurt him and Lola, but pulverized them.

"Okay..." After a deep breath, she stood, wiping her palms on the thighs of black slacks. "If you won't come to me…" When she slipped her arms around his waist, his body instinctively craved more.

No, no, no. He refused to let her in, which is why he backed a safe distance away.

"I'm sorry, Brady. I made horrible mistakes. I wasn't ready for another commitment, but I'm also not ready for you to be out of my life."

"Are you even listening to what you're saying? You left me and my little girl standing at the altar—no, wait." Marching over to her, finger in her face, he said, "You didn't even give us the dignity of just quietly telling me it was over. You freakin' ran like I'd set you on fire. Do you have any idea what that felt like? And then there was sitting around the most romantic beach house in the world with my eight-year-old, playing Monopoly and Clue."

"How many ways can I apologize?" Holding her arms out, she let them fall with a slap against her thighs. "I screwed up. Made the worst mistake of my life. I'm so, so sorry. I've been seeing a therapist, and it's been life-changing. I even flew to Seattle, and then here without being tranquilized. I don't want to rely on pills for the rest of my life. I want to learn to deal with my pain. But I need your help. I need you to believe in me, and tell me everything's going to be okay."

Cupping her cheeks and brushing away her tears with his thumbs, he said, "Don't you think that's exactly what I want to do? What I've always wanted to do? But, Steph, I don't know if I can. Do you realize that not once during our engagement, did you tell me you loved me? I know it's a small thing. Three stupid words, but you seem incapable of saying them. I need a woman who can tell me. Not because I'm insecure, but because I'm worth it."

"You are," she said, taking him by his wrists and kissing his palms and fingers. "I love you—and Lola—so much. I'm sorry for not saying it sooner, but I was afraid. Losing Michael changed me. I was so scared—of everything."

"Don't you think I'm scared? What if, like Clarissa, you leave me, taking the twins with you? Life doesn't come with guarantees."

Laughing and crying at the same time, she said, "My therapist tells me that."

"She—or he—is right."

"She."

"Whatever." Kissing her full on her beautiful mouth, he said, "You have to realize that all we can do is surround ourselves with people we love and hope for the best. And, Stephanie, if you'd just open your heart, you'd see that's what we were—could be—together. The best."

Holding on to him for dear life, Stephanie couldn't have agreed more.

Epilogue

"Steph!" Brady shouted in front of the hall closet. It was their six-month wedding anniversary and movers would be there any minute.

Toddlers, Michaela and Melanie, had hold of his legs and they were covered in something sticky and red.

"Ladies…" he said with a groan "…did your sister leave the strawberry jam out again?"

"Uh-huh," they said in unison with identical mischievous grins. "Lola in twouble." The phrase was their favorite.

As for their older sister, she didn't much like it.

"Steph!" he repeated. "Nobody packed the hall closet!"

"Go for it," she said, leaving their bedroom with a box in her arms only to enter the nursery.

"What have you been doing?" he asked, trailing after her with the twins attached to his legs like cherubic leeches.

"What's it look like?" She flashed him the contents of her box. Shoes. He should've known. When they'd first met, she couldn't have cared less about fashion, but since Lola's first summer with them, she'd turned into a mall rat just like his daughter.

"Eeeuw," she said, looking at the girls. "Did Lola by chance leave out the jam?"

"Lola in twouble," the twins said again.

Shaking his head, Brady asked, "Think they were more fun before learning to talk?"

Steph kissed him before tackling the girls' dresser. Their new house was in Seattle. Only a mile from Clarissa and Vince's. Brady and Steph both wanted to spend as much time as possible with Lola. With the twins not anywhere near starting school, this was the logical time for the move. Helen bought the pastry shop and when the girls did enter kindergarten, Steph planned on starting a new store that also featured homemade candy. In the meantime, she seemed excited about spending loads of time with all of their girls and working on their modern monstrosity of a fixer-upper.

"Sweetie," Steph said once she'd finished, giving him the smile he was never strong enough to resist. "Would you *please* pack the closet? You don't even have to be neat. Just throw it all in a box."

With a good-natured groan, he molded his fingers to twin blond heads. "Come on, kiddos. Looks like Mom's putting us to work."

"Thank you!" Stephanie hollered from the nursery.

"What's this?" Lola asked, making more of a mess in the closet than there had already been.

"What's what?" he asked.

She'd found a blue gift box and removed the lid. After peeking at the contents, she said, "Oops. Think I might've found your Christmas and birthday gift."

"Let me see." He easily took the box.

"Momma Steph's gonna be mad at you," she said.

"I'll just take a quick look. Don't tell."

"Don't tell what?" Steph asked, emerging from the nursery.

"Nothing." Brady hid the box behind his back.

"Let me see."

Wrestling for it, he finally resorted to holding it over his wife's head.

"You're awful!"

Laughing, he said, "I'd rather be awful than stubby."

"Now, you're gonna get it." She gave his chest a playful pummel.

"Lola in twouble!" The laughing twins jumped up and down. "Lola in twouble!"

"What'd I do?" the preteen complained. To the twins, she said, "You two need psychiatric help." Rolling her eyes at her dad and stepmother's antics, she put her iPod's earbuds back in and headed for the kitchen.

When Brady finally lowered the box, Stephanie gasped. "Where did you find that?"

He shrugged. "Lola fished it out of the closet."

"I looked everywhere…"

"Since I found it, can I keep it?" he asked, hoping she'd agree.

"At least sit down," she urged, leading him to the sofa. "It's a pretty big deal."

"Now I'm really excited." To the twins, he said, "How about letting Daddy go? Then you can find Lola and see if she's getting in trouble."

"I heard that!" Lola shouted from the kitchen.

The twins took off in that direction.

Seated beside Steph, Brady finally removed the box's lid, and got his first look inside. After reading the inscription, "Love is the Greatest Adventure," he looked to Stephanie. "Is this for real?"

Tears shining in her eyes, she nodded. "Like it?"

He clutched the autographed, leather-bound book to his heart. "*Like* doesn't come close to describing how amazing this is. Where did you get it?"

"Remember our first Christmas? When I dragged you back to my room to give you a present I'd bought at auction?"

"This was it?"

She nodded. "After the wedding, I found it, but then it somehow got misplaced again."

"Sweetheart," he said, still clutching the gift, "I can't begin to tell you what this means. That all the way back then, you loved me enough to remember something so insignificant as my idolizing Amelia Earhart."

"Don't you get it?" she asked, kissing him square on his lips. "When it comes to you, Mr. McGuire, there's nothing insignificant. You're my world. And I love you."

Though he may have had his doubts in the beginning, the more he was with Stephanie, the more crazy in love he fell. Only in their house, with goldfish and at least part of the year, three kids, and an always hiding kitten, heavy emphasis needed to be placed on crazy!

Harlequin offers a romance for every mood!
See below for a sneak peek from our
suspense romance line
Silhouette® Romantic Suspense.
Introducing HER HERO IN HIDING *by*
New York Times *bestselling author Rachel Lee.*

Kay Young returned to woozy consciousness to find that she was lying on a soft sofa beneath a heap of quilts near a cheerfully burning fire. When she tried to move, however, everything hurt, and she groaned.

At once she heard a sound, then a stranger with a hard, harsh face was squatting beside her. "Shh," he said softly. "You're safe here. I promise."

"I have to go," she said weakly, struggling against pain. "He'll find me. He can't find me."

"Easy, lady," he said quietly. "You're hurt. No one's going to find you here."

"He will," she said desperately, terror clutching at her insides. "He always finds me!"

"Easy," he said again. "There's a blizzard outside. No one's getting here tonight, not even the doctor. I know, because I tried."

"Doctor? I don't need a doctor! I've got to get away."

"There's nowhere to go tonight," he said levelly. "And if I thought you could stand, I'd take you to a window and show you."

But even as she tried once more to pull away the quilts, she remembered something else: this man had been gentle when he'd found her beside the road, even when she had kicked and clawed. He hadn't hurt her.

Terror receded just a bit. She looked at him and detected signs of true concern there.

The terror eased another notch and she let her head sag on the pillow. "He always finds me," she whispered.

"Not here. Not tonight. That much I can guarantee."

*Will Kay's mysterious rescuer protect her
from her worst fears?*
Find out in HER HERO IN HIDING *by*
New York Times *bestselling author Rachel Lee.*
Available June 2010,
only from Silhouette® Romantic Suspense.

HARLEQUIN® *Romance*®

GIRLS' *Weekend in* VEGAS

Four friends, four dream weddings!

On a girly weekend in Las Vegas, best friends Alex, Molly, Serena and Jayne are supposed to just have fun and forget men, but they end up meeting their perfect matches! Will the love they find in Vegas stay in Vegas?

Find out in this sassy, fun and wildly romantic miniseries all about love and friendship!

Saving Cinderella! by MYRNA MACKENZIE
Available June

Vegas Pregnancy Surprise by SHIRLEY JUMP
Available July

Inconveniently Wed! by JACKIE BRAUN
Available August

Wedding Date with the Best Man
by MELISSA MCCLONE
Available September

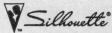

ROMANTIC
SUSPENSE

Sparked by Danger, Fueled by Passion.

NEW YORK TIMES AND *USA TODAY*
BESTSELLING AUTHOR

RACHEL LEE

BRINGS YOU AN ALL-NEW
CONARD COUNTY: THE NEXT GENERATION SAGA!

After finding the injured Kay Young on a deserted country
road Clint Ardmore learns that she is not only being hunted
by a serial killer, but is also three months pregnant.
He is determined to protect them—even if it means
forgoing the solitude that he has come to appreciate.
But will Clint grow fond of having an attractive woman
occupy his otherwise empty ranch?

Find out in

Her Hero in Hiding

Available June 2010 wherever books are sold.

Visit Silhouette Books at www.eHarlequin.com

REQUEST YOUR FREE BOOKS!
2 FREE NOVELS PLUS 2 FREE GIFTS!

HARLEQUIN®

American Romance®

Love, Home & Happiness!

YES! Please send me 2 FREE Harlequin® American Romance® novels and my 2 FREE gifts (gifts are worth about $10). After receiving them, if I don't wish to receive any more books, I can return the shipping statement marked "cancel." If I don't cancel, I will receive 4 brand-new novels every month and be billed just $4.24 per book in the U.S. or $4.99 per book in Canada. That's a saving of at least 15% off the cover price! It's quite a bargain! Shipping and handling is just 50¢ per book.* I understand that accepting the 2 free books and gifts places me under no obligation to buy anything. I can always return a shipment and cancel at any time. Even if I never buy another book from Harlequin, the two free books and gifts are mine to keep forever.

154/354 HDN E5LG

Name _____ (PLEASE PRINT)

Address _____ Apt. #

City _____ State/Prov. _____ Zip/Postal Code

Signature (if under 18, a parent or guardian must sign)

Mail to the Harlequin Reader Service:
IN U.S.A.: P.O. Box 1867, Buffalo, NY 14240-1867
IN CANADA: P.O. Box 609, Fort Erie, Ontario L2A 5X3

Not valid for current subscribers to Harlequin® American Romance® books.

Want to try two free books from another line?
Call 1-800-873-8635 or visit www.morefreebooks.com.

* Terms and prices subject to change without notice. Prices do not include applicable taxes. N.Y. residents add applicable sales tax. Canadian residents will be charged applicable provincial taxes and GST. Offer not valid in Quebec. This offer is limited to one order per household. All orders subject to approval. Credit or debit balances in a customer's account(s) may be offset by any other outstanding balance owed by or to the customer. Please allow 4 to 6 weeks for delivery. Offer available while quantities last.

Your Privacy: Harlequin is committed to protecting your privacy. Our Privacy Policy is available online at www.eHarlequin.com or upon request from the Reader Service. From time to time we make our lists of customers available to reputable third parties who may have a product or service of interest to you. If you would prefer we not share your name and address, please check here. ☐

Help us get it right—We strive for accurate, respectful and relevant communications. To clarify or modify your communication preferences, visit us at www.ReaderService.com/consumerchoice.

HAR10R

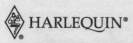

Love Inspired

Bestselling author

JILLIAN HART

brings you another heartwarming story
from

the
GRANGER FAMILY RANCH

Rancher Justin Granger hasn't seen his high school sweetheart
since she rode out of town with his heart. Now she's back, with
sadness in her eyes, seeking a job as his cook and housekeeper.
He agrees but is determined to avoid her…until he discovers
that her big dream has always been him!

The Rancher's Promise

*Available June
wherever books are sold.*

Steeple
Hill®

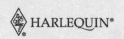

HARLEQUIN®

Showcase

On sale May 11, 2010

Reader favorites from the most talented voices in romance

Save $1.00 on the purchase of 1 or more Harlequin® Showcase books.

SAVE $1.00 on the purchase of 1 or more Harlequin® Showcase books.

Coupon expires Oct 31, 2010. Redeemable at participating retail outlets.
Limit one coupon per purchase. Valid in the U.S.A. and Canada only.

52609015

5 65373 00076 2 (8100)0 11651

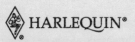
HARLEQUIN®

COMING NEXT MONTH

Available June 8, 2010

#1309 THE SHERIFF AND THE BABY
Babies & Bachelors USA
C.C. Coburn

#1310 WALKER: THE RODEO LEGEND
The Codys: The First Family of Rodeo
Rebecca Winters

#1311 THE BEST MAN IN TEXAS
Tanya Michaels

#1312 SECOND CHANCE HERO
Shelley Galloway

www.eHarlequin.com